Victoria Parker

—

To Claim His Heir by Christmas

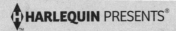
HARLEQUIN PRESENTS®

Recycling programs
for this product may
not exist in your area.

ISBN-13: 978-0-373-13302-4

To Claim His Heir by Christmas

First North American Publication 2014

Copyright © 2014 by Victoria Parker

Printed in U.S.A.

www.Harlequin.com

"I have to go home today. I have to go back to Arunthia, and I need you to take me—like you promised."

He sat up in one lithe, rippling movement, like a panther uncurling, and pushed his tousled hair back from his forehead. "No, Luciana, don't say that." His husky, lethargic voice grew stronger, firmer. "You belong here with me. There's no reason for you to go back."

Luciana swallowed around the searing burn in her throat. "But there is, Thane. Someone is there that I can't leave. *Ever.*"

His expression darkened, and she felt a frisson of fear. Flinched when he suddenly ripped the sheet from his body, vaulted from the bed and spun on her. "You love this person?"

"Yes," she said, her voice cracking under pressure. "I love him more than life itself."

His eyes grew furious, dark as rain-laden thunderclouds. And she knew it was only going to get worse. This, she realized, was merely the beginning. God help her.

"Who do you love?" he demanded.

You can do this, Luciana. For him—for your son. Thane will rip your heart from your chest, but this is not about you. It is about the little boy you love and his father. You are doing it for them. They deserve this from you. Do it. Do it.

"Please don't hate me, Thane," she whispered, begging him. "I was only trying to do the right thing. I was scared. I only wanted him to be safe—"

His beauty took on a terrifying, dangerous edge. "Who, Luciana?" He flung his arms wide. "Who do you love?"

"Our son."

All about the author...
Victoria Parker

VICTORIA PARKER's first love was a dashing heroic fox named Robin Hood. Then came the powerful, suave Mr. Darcy, then Lady Chatterley's rugged lover...and the list goes on. Thinking she must be an unfaithful sort of girl, but ever the optimist, she relentlessly pursued her Mr. Literary Right and eventually found him lying between the cool, crisp sheets of a Harlequin® romance. Her obsession was born.

If only real life was just as easy...

Alas, against the advice of her beloved English teacher to cultivate her writer's muse, she chased the corporate dream and acquired various uninspiring job titles *and* a flesh-and-blood hero before she surrendered to that persistent voice and penned her first Harlequin® romance. It turns out creating havoc for feisty heroines and devilish heroes truly *is* the best job in the world.

Victoria now lives out her own happy-ever-after in the northeast of England with her alpha exec and their two children—a masterly charmer in the making and, apparently, the next Disney Princess. Believing sleep is highly overrated, she often writes until 3:00 a.m., ignores the housework (much to her husband's dismay) and still loves nothing more than getting cozy with a romance novel. In her spare time she enjoys dabbling with interior design, discovering far-flung destinations and getting into mischief with her rather wonderful extended family.

Other titles by Victoria Parker available in ebook:

THE ULTIMATE REVENGE
 (The 21st Century Gentleman's Club)
THE WOMAN SENT TO TAME HIM
A REPUTATION TO UPHOLD
PRINCESS IN THE IRON MASK

To Claim His Heir by Christmas

To ADP. I thank the fates for you every day.

To my fabulous editor, Kathryn Cheshire, who suffered through the initial drafts with endless patience and compassion as I stumbled through a dark time in my life. I'm so very grateful for your insight, your understanding and most of all, your faith in me. The day I hold this book in my hand, I shall only think of how you made it bigger, better, so much stronger. Thank you. For everything.

And finally to my readers.
Especially those of you who wrote and asked me to pen another Arunthian tale. I hope you enjoy Luciana and Thane's story and as promised, you'll get to say hi to Claudia and Lucas along the way.

CHAPTER ONE

HE WAS GOING to propose. Any minute now.

It was every little girl's dream. A handsome man, one of the most beautiful she'd ever seen, sat opposite her at an intimate table for two, with a velvet box nestled in his inside pocket. Aristocracy, no less. The suave Savile Row sophisticate who was Viscount Augustus. The man who'd set the scene so superbly.

Dimly lit chandeliers cast a seductive romantic ambience throughout the room of the critically acclaimed restaurant, where Michelin chefs were famous for creating masterpieces of haute cuisine. Open fires crackled and crystal tinkled as exorbitantly priced champagne flowed, poured into flutes in an amber rush of opulent effervescence. And beyond the wide plate-glass windows lay the majestic vista of the Tarentaise Valley—Savoie, bathing in the rose-pink wash of dusk, its white-capped mountains towering from the earth like watchful sentinels over the exclusive lavish ski resort of Pur Luxe.

Stunning. Awe-inspiring. The stage was set.

All that was left were the words.

And Princess Luciana Valentia Thyssen Verbault was paralysed with dread.

Please, God, please get me out of this somehow...

There is no way out, Luce. Not only do you have a duty to your people but a deal is a deal. And you made one with the devil himself.

Lord, she hated her father right now. *'Go to the Alps,'* he'd said. *'Take a few days to think things over, get your head together.'*

Luciana had taken in his seemingly sincere autocratic face, paler since she'd last seen him as his health continued to deteriorate, and thought, yes, a few days to ponder. After all, she'd thought, she had years before her coronation, plenty of room to breathe, to barter for more time. But, as the saying went: Men plan. Fates laugh.

King Henri of Arunthia was being pushed by his doctors to retire. So she'd come to inhale the invigorating crisp air, to infuse her mind with solace. Reassess. Come up with a strategy where matrimony wouldn't equate to losing the only person she lived for. What her father *hadn't* said was that he was dropping her smack-bang in the midst of her worst nightmare by sending Augustus to seal the deal.

She supposed she should have seen it coming. Avoiding the Viscount via any means possible since her return home from China three weeks ago obviously hadn't worked a jot. All she'd done was delay the inevitable.

You can run but you can't hide. Wasn't that what they said?

Truth was, for so long she'd been living on borrowed time, wishing with all her heart that time would miraculously stand still. But time, as she'd soon realised, waited for no man. Let alone a woman as desperate as she was to avoid the ticking clock.

Now she would pay the ultimate price for bartering with her father five too short years ago. Five years of living a normal existence, well hidden in her sanctuary near Hong Kong. Five years of latitude and liberty in exchange for total compliance—starting now.

'Luciana? Is the *filet* not to your liking, *querida*?'

Her eyelashes fluttered as she fought the urge to squeeze them shut. Pretend she was anywhere but here. *Querida...* Lord, she wished he wouldn't call her that. Wished too that she could extinguish the heat banked in his blue eyes. Hadn't he had enough carnal relations for one afternoon? She almost asked him. If he'd enjoyed the brunette in his suite. The one who'd answered his door half naked and ravaged. But the truth was she couldn't care less. It was the endearments she loathed. They hinted at affection and love and there would be none in this marriage. On either side.

He was playing a part, though, wasn't he? She wondered, then, if he was going to get down on one knee. While she sincerely hoped not, he was a virtuoso at playing the press and they'd want the fairy story.

Fairy story. Yeah, right. A fool's dream. Like so many others that taunted her day and night.

'It's wonderful, thank you,' she said, attempting another small mouthful even as her stomach roiled.

It could be the best *filet mignon* in the world and it would still taste like black ash. Though no one would ever know it. Trained by the best, she was the perfect picture of elegant refinement. Graceful to a fault.

'Good. I want tonight to be perfect,' he said softly. Slick and skilful.

Luciana whipped out the serene smile she'd perfected since the cradle—not too bright or flashy, nor too dull. *Just perfect*, as her mother would say. Neglecting to add the tiny detail that it would strip her throat raw every time she faked it.

'I want tonight to be perfect.'

Guilt trickled through the turbulent maelstrom of emotions warring for dominance in her chest. He was trying, wasn't he?

Of course he is—he wants a throne of his own. Of course he's pulling out every weapon in his cultivated arsenal.

Still, it wasn't his fault that the 'arranged marriage' part of her conditioning hadn't quite taken root. It wasn't his fault that she dreamed of another. It wasn't his fault that she had a taste for dark and dangerous.

Yes, and look what trouble that landed you in. Surely you've learned your lesson by now?

And Augustus was good-looking. Very handsome, in fact. Sandy blond hair artfully shorn and midnight-blue eyes. He had women after him in their droves. Yet he was her duty—tall and fair. The man she'd been ordered to wed. And from there to his bed.

A phantom knife sliced through her stomach and instinctively she bowed forward to ease the lancing pain… Then she forced her poise to kick in, reached gingerly for her glass and poured the amber liquid down her throat. Maybe if she got tipsy enough she'd have enough anaesthetic on board to say yes without shattering into a million pieces.

Flute back to the table, Luciana picked up her fork to push the tenderised beef around her gold-rimmed plate on the off-chance that he'd reach for her hand again. Once this evening was more than enough.

Would she ever get used to his touch? It was nothing like when *he'd* touched her. Nothing like the wickedly high jolt of electricity that had surged through her veins, or the blaze of her blood creating a raging inferno inside her.

Stop! For the love of God, Luciana, stop.

Problem was, as always, she found it impossible to halt the flow. The fiery rush of memories. Memories of a man who'd given her a gift to last a lifetime.

Pain and secrecy thumped inside her ribs like a dark heart. Because no one could know. No one could ever, *ever* know.

Princesses of the realm, first in line to the throne, were *not* meant to disgrace themselves by breaking free of their dutiful chains. Not meant to alter their appearance beyond recognition to avoid the paparazzi and go to rock concerts in Zurich dressed like a hippy, doling out false names. Not meant to fall in love…no, *lust* at first sight and have wild, passionate love affairs. They especially weren't supposed to have them with Arunthia's enemy. Not that she'd known exactly who he was when they'd met.

Such an ironic twist of fate. One she would have reduced to a dream if she didn't hold and squeeze and hug and kiss the living proof of her reckless walk on the wild side every single day. Yet, despite it all—despite knowing she'd given her innocence to a treacherous, dangerous man—she could never, *would* never regret it. Because her first and only lover had given her a gift that was the single most brilliant, bright spark of joy in her world...her son.

Discreetly she sneaked a peek at the mobile phone hidden in her lap to see if Natanael's goodnight text had come through. Nothing. She stifled the melancholy of missing him by picturing him playing happily with her sister Claudia and baby Isabelle, while Lucas watched on adoringly, protectively. Possessively.

At times it physically hurt to look at them. The perfect family. So deeply, devotedly in love. Their beautiful marriage was eons away from the unions she was used to. Luciana hadn't known such a thing existed. She would do anything for that. Pay any price.

Envy, thick and poignant, pierced her chest with a sweet, sharp ache and she cursed herself for feeling that way. Wanting what she couldn't have. Plunging lower than the black trench of despair she'd dug beneath her own feet. On the verge of letting loose the scream that was irrevocably bottled up inside her.

Come on, Luce. You know happiness isn't written in the cards for a royal firstborn. Only duty.

Luciana tried to swallow and block the lash of repercussions her trip down the aisle would provoke before anguish swept her mind away on a tide of insanity.

Stop this! You're protecting him—just as you've always done.

But how was she ever going to leave her heart? The person she needed in order to breathe, as if he were the very air itself? Her gorgeous little boy.

Claudia had sworn she'd save him from the oppressive walls of Arunthe Palace, love him as Luciana did until she could figure out a way for them to be together always. As Queen she'd have more power. She would think of something. She *had* to.

In the meantime Luciana would always be near—but what about his tub time, and the way he liked to be tucked tight and snug into bed? Luciana wanted to run his bath with his favourite bubbles that made his tender skin smell sweet. And what about when he called for her in the night when he was having bad dreams? *She* wanted to hold him when he was scared.

The thought of him asking for her and her not being there… It tormented her mind. How she was going to explain it all to him she had no idea. And how was she going to leave Natanael behind if this man dragged her to his family estate in Northern Arunthia?

So tell him. Tell him. He might understand. Support you. Help you.

This man? No. No, she didn't trust him not to betray her confidence. Didn't trust anyone.

You made a deal, Luciana. Now you pay.

Ah, yes, a deal made in naïve, youthful folly. In desperation such as she'd never known. A pact etched in her mind like an effigy on a tombstone. A shiver ghosted over her as she was haunted by the past…

'Please…please, Father. I can't do it. I can't get rid of him.'
She knew he was small, so small inside her, but she couldn't take him away, she couldn't give him up. She couldn't.

'Luciana, you are not married. You will bring disgrace on us all. You are the heiress to the throne and the father of the child you carry is an enemy of this nation. Do you

forget his assassination attempt? On me? He is a traitor to the crown.'

'Yes, but I didn't know who he was. I—'

'If this man ever discovered your child's existence he could use him as a pawn to gain power over us. He could take Arunthia. And do you honestly want his Satan of an uncle getting his hands on your son? We have avoided war for sixty years—do you want your people to live in tyranny as those in Galancia do?'

'No, no. But...no one need ever know. I could go away for a while. Please, I'm begging you. Pleading with you... Let me keep him.'

The King's deep sigh filled the oppressive air stifling his office and she teetered on the precipice of throwing her pride to the gale and plunging to her knees.

Then he said, *'Five years, Luciana. Five years of freedom. That is all I will give you. But the world must never know he is yours because Thane must never, ever find him. You will never be able to claim him as your son and heir. Do you understand me?'*

'Yes. Yes, I understand,' she said—wild, frenzied, frantic. Unthinking of the consequences of what she was agreeing to. So desperate she would have sold her soul in that moment.

'You will be hidden well in the Far East, and in five years you will return to take the throne and do your duty. You will marry, Luciana, am I clear?'

'Yes—yes, I swear it. I'll do whatever you want. Just let me have him.'

His steely eyes were clouded with disappointment and grief and sorrow. That gaze was telling her she would rue this day, this bargain.

Luciana ignored it. As long as her son got to take his first breath, got to walk upon the earth and live life to the full, without the constraints of duty like a noose around his neck, she would make a deal with the devil himself. And so she did.

* * *

Augustus's voice shattered her bleak reflection and she tuned back in to the chatter that fluttered around them in a hushed din.

All she had to do was remember that her happiness came second to Natanael's safety. And she *would* keep him safe if it was the last thing she did.

'Luciana? Would you like coffee and dessert or…?'

Or…? Lord, not now. Not when she was falling apart at the seams. She wasn't ready to hear those words. Not yet. *Not ever.*

She felt powerless. Completely out of control. Like a puppet on a string.

The room began to spin.

'Yes, thank you, that would be wonderful,' she said, her voice thankfully calm and emotion-free as she plastered a cringe-worthy beatific smile on her face.

Coffee. Crème brulée. That would buy her another twenty minutes, surely.

Panic fisted her heart as the tick of the clock pounded in her ears. Tick-tock. Tick-tock.

The walls loomed, closing in around her, crushing her lungs.

Calm down, Luce. What are you going to do—hyperventilate and pass out? Make a total fool of yourself?

She needed air. She couldn't breathe.

'I'm sorry—please excuse me. I think I need…' To go out on the balcony? No, no, no, he'd follow her and drop to one knee, she knew. 'To visit the restroom. I'll only be a few minutes.'

After all that she realised he wasn't listening. Someone on the other side of the room had caught his eye, and Luciana frowned as his lightly tanned face stained a ghastly shade of grey.

'Augustus? Are you all right? Did you hear what I said?'

Slowly he shook his head. 'I do not believe it. Luciana,

you will never guess who is dining in this very room. I had no idea. Your father will be most displeased. I am so sorry...'

He was *sorry*? Ah, wonderful. One of his women, no doubt. The buxom brunette from earlier, come to ruin his perfect proposal? She didn't want to know. It was her parents' marriage all over again. No doubt she'd be faced with his mistresses most mornings too.

Well, that's better than you warming his bed, isn't it?

Anything was better than that.

'Don't worry about it, Augustus. Your secret is safe with me.' Her father wouldn't care less who the man whored with. There was more likelihood of mutual backslapping. 'I'll be back soon.'

Ignoring her, on he went. 'Of all the places in all the world...'

Luciana bit into her bottom lip, stifling the impulse to run like a world class sprinter. Praying for this evening to be over. Praying someone would rescue her from this nightmare. Before the truth escaped on the scream that was building gradually, inexorably, and she single-handedly destroyed the very life she was trying to protect.

'Of all the places in all the world... What an unpleasant surprise.'

His cousin, Seve, who was seated to his right at the oval dining table, leaned his upper body sideways in an effort to be discreet.

'I can see the sweat beading on his upper lip from here. It's your old pal from that exclusive rich joint you were sent to in Zurich. Viscount Augustus.'

Prince Thane of Galancia deflected the gut-punch the word *Zurich* evoked and sneered. 'He was no *pal* of mine.'

For the one disastrous university term Thane had attended after his father's death the Viscount had caused him no end of trouble—which he'd soon discovered was a horrendously bad idea—and subsequently shaken in his shoes every time

he looked Thane's way. Which had pleased Thane no end.
It meant he'd generally kept a vast distance.

He couldn't abide the man. Augustus was a wolf in
sheep's clothing. Polished until every inch of him gleamed,
he was a silver-tongued bureaucrat with sly eyes and a
treacherous mind.

Seve smirked as if Thane had said the words out loud
and he'd found it highly amusing. 'What's more, he's dining
with none other than Princess Luciana of Arunthia. One of
Henri's stuck-up brood.'

Thane resisted the urge to growl. 'Then they belong together.' A match made in heaven. 'How do you know it's
definitely her? Last I heard, she lived abroad.'

He couldn't remember the last time he'd seen a photograph of *any* of them. Recent intel was off his radar, since
he had zero interest in becoming embroiled with his uncle's
ongoing bitter feud with the house of Verbault. He'd made
that mistake ten years ago, in his father's day. Had the scars
and the bitter aftertaste to prove it. Nowadays every time he
thought of that varmint Henri a seizure of antagonistic emotion diseased his mind, so the less he heard or saw of the entire family the better. Besides, his every waking moment was
spent deflecting blows from the latest fiasco in Galancia.

'I *know* because the two of them having fun on the slopes
made the French headlines this morning. Rumour has it she's
newly returned from Hong Kong, due to take the crown
any day.'

Thane would have predicted a snowball in hell before he
felt envy for a Verbault, but right then envy was definitely
the evil he was up against. He wanted *his* crown. Taken
from the hands of his uncle and placed in his own, where it
should be. Before the man caused his people further damage. Four years... It seemed eons away, and his patience was
wearing perilously thin.

He thrust his fingers through his hair and tucked some
of the long, wayward strands behind his ear. 'It isn't hard

to work out what Augustus wants. The vapid Viscount has always been an ambitious sleaze with illusions of grandeur.'

Seve chuckled darkly. 'Very true. Although I will say that marriage to her will be no chore for him. Look at her. By God, she's absolutely stunning.'

Thane couldn't care less if she was Cleopatra. She was still a Verbault. Granted, he refused to get snarled up in that age-old vendetta again, but he wasn't ignorant or blind to the reasoning for it. Verbault greed had once crippled a vulnerable Galancia, and rebuilding its former glory was an ongoing battle. Forgiveness would never be proffered. So the day he aligned with one of them would be the day he rode bareback with the Four Horsemen of the Apocalypse.

Seve, meanwhile, was still staring her way. Smitten. Practically drooling. 'I don't think I've ever seen a more beautiful woman in my life.'

'That's saying something, considering how many you've bedded,' Thane incised sardonically.

His cousin, his second in command, his best friend—the only person he would ever trust—shrugged his wide shoulders. 'Wouldn't do you any harm to get laid either, cousin. Come on—I didn't drag you here just to hurtle down the black slopes all day.'

He knew fine well what Seve had dragged him here for. All work and no play made Thane a dull, arrogant ass, apparently—and for a minute or three he had considered it. But when the redhead sitting to his right had appeared from nowhere he'd turned to stone. Unable even to contemplate getting close to another woman. In fact, if she touched his arm one more time...

Dios, didn't she know he was dangerous? That his blood ran black and his heart was dead? That he was more powerful and more feared than any other man in Europe? Surely his scars were enough to give her a clue?

Maybe he should give the mindless female a lesson in Princes of Galancia. Top of the list: do not touch.

He *hated* being touched. Didn't want anyone close to him. Ever again. While getting beaten to a pulp couldn't possibly hurt him any longer, it was the softer stuff that was more dangerous. One taste and he might very well crave it. Long for more of it. Glut himself on it. Live for it. Every touch. Every caress. Every kiss. Until it was taken away, as it inevitably would be. Leaving him empty. Aching. *Feeling.* Weak. And the dark Prince of Galancia could not afford to be weak. Not again. When he was weak he took his eye off the ball and everything went to hell.

Thane reached for his tumbler of rare single malt, his hand stalling in mid-air as an army of ants marched across his nape. Instinct born from a childhood in the barracks made him turn to peer over his right shoulder. Past the garish pine trees smothered in red ribbons and gold baubles, declaring the onslaught of the festive season. *How quaint. How pointless.*

Ah, yes, there was Augustus. Averting his gaze like an errant schoolboy. No woman with him—not that Thane could see.

But what he *did* see was a striking, statuesque blonde walking in the direction of the hallway that led to the restrooms. No. Not blonde at all. Her rich, decadent shower of loose tousled waves reminded him of a dark bronze. Like new-fallen acorns.

Now, *she* was beautiful. And that thought was so incredulous, so foreign, that he felt a tingle of something suspiciously close to shock.

His avid gaze locked on its target, his usual two-second scan turning into a drawn-out visual seduction, and he trailed his eyes over the low scooped neck of the black sheath that hugged her feminine curves. Lingered on the lapels of her long white dress coat, frisking and teasing all that flawless golden flesh.

A faint frown creased her brow and Thane narrowed his

eyes as she raised one hand and rubbed over the seam of her lips with the pad of her thumb.

A pleasurable shiver of recognition rippled over his skin and his entire body prickled with an unfathomable heat.

Ana used to do that. Stroke her mouth that way. When he'd asked her why, she'd said it likely came from sucking her thumb when she was a little girl. Thane had smiled and cracked some joke about her still liking things in her mouth, and she'd proceeded to prove him right. Many times over...

The brazen fires of lust swirled through his groin, and when the woman inhaled deeply—the action pushing those full, high breasts of surreal temptation to swell against the thin silk of her dress—ferocious heat speared through his veins until he flushed from top to toe.

It couldn't be. Could it? His Ana? Here in the Alps? No, surely not. Ana's hair was sable-black. Her body far more slender.

Look at me, he ordered. *Turn around,* he demanded. *Now.*

And she did. Or rather she spared a glance across the room in his direction, then wrestled with her poise, giving her head a little shake.

Thane's hands balled in frustration. But he kept watching as she reached the slightly secluded archway leading to the restrooms. Alone, doubtless believing she was unseen, she tipped her head back, glancing skyward as if praying to God, and graced him with the elegant curve of her smooth throat.

Another flashback hit with crystalline precision—*his* woman, arching off the bed, back bowed as she seized in rapture beneath him, inarticulate cries pouring from her swollen ruby-red mouth. And for the first time in his life—or maybe the second—his insides started to shake. *Shake.*

Dios, was his mind playing tricks on him? *Months* he had searched for her. For that trail of sable hair, that mesmerising beauty mark above her full lips, those clothes that harked of dark blood, a roaming gypsy. No stone had been unturned in Zurich, since that was where they had met, where she had *claimed* to live. Torturous years of not knowing whether she was dead or alive. Living with the grief. The ferocious anger and self-hate that choked him at the notion that he might not have protected her. That she could have been taken from him because of who he was.

He blinked and she was gone. Disappeared once again. And before he knew it he'd shoved his chair backwards with an emphatic scrape.

'Thane?'

'Restroom,' he said, and followed the dark blonde, his heart stampeding through his chest.

Thane thrust the double doors wide, then took a sharp right down the first corridor—and came to a dead end. A swift turn about and he flung open the double doors to the wraparound balcony. Empty.

Impatience thrummed inside him. The notion of being thwarted tore at his guts. He closed the doors with a quick click, turned and—

Slam.

'Ooof.' He ran straight into another body so hard and fast he had to grab hold of her upper arms to stop her from careening backwards and crashing to the floor.

'I…I'm sorry. I wasn't looking where I was going. Please…'

Just the sound of her voice washed clean rain over him. She was breathless, winded, clutching his lapels as if he was her life raft in the darkest, most turbulent storm.

'Please. I need to…'

That soft, husky whimper flung him back in time, sent electricity sizzling over every inch of his skin. And the way she'd jolted—he would hazard a guess she'd felt it too.

Stumbling back a step, she jacked up her chin and their gazes caught, clashed…

Madre de Dios!

'Ana?'

Brandy-gold eyes flared up at him as bee-stung lips

parted with a gasp. And for the endless moments they stared at one another she seemed to pelt through a tumult of emotions. He could virtually see them flicker over her exquisite face. Fancied each one mirrored his own. She was astounded. Bewildered. Likely in denial. Half convinced she was hallucinating. And all the while Thane drank her in as if he'd been dying of thirst and his pulse-rate tripled to create a sonic boom in his ears.

He wanted to take her in his arms. Bury his fingers into the luxurious fall of her hair. Hold her tightly to him. Despite the internal screech of warning not to touch, not become ensnared in her again.

Thane swallowed around the emotional grenade lodged in his throat. 'Ana, where have you been? I looked for you. What happened? I…'

Unable to wait a second longer, he reached out—but she staggered back another step; her brow pinched with pain.

'No. No! Don't touch me. I'm sorry. You must be mistaking me for someone else. I…'

That pain morphed into something like fear and punched him in the gut.

'Please excuse me,' she said, and she made to duck past him.

His confusion made his cat-like reflexes take a second too long to kick in.

'Ana? What are you talking about?'

Why was she scared of him? He didn't like it. Not one bit. Everyone else? Yes. Her? No.

A man emerged from around the corner and when Thane recognised Augustus he almost swung his fist in the other man's face. Though at the last second he thought better of it. His word, he'd been told, was vehement enough. Consequently he opened his mouth to deliver a curt command but the Viscount beat him to the punch.

'Luciana? Are you all right, *querida*?'

Luciana? Hold on a minute… *Querida*?

What the *hell* was going on?

'Luciana? Is this man bothering you?'

Thane whipped around to face him. 'Back off, Augustus,' he ground out, jabbing his finger at the other man while he tried to think around the incessant clatter in his brain. 'And while you are doing that, if you know what is good for you, turn around and *walk away*.'

Augustus paled beneath his tanned skin, nodded and went to do just that. But not before he motioned to Ana with a jerk of his chin. Or was it Luciana? *Dios*, Thane felt as if his head was splitting in two.

'Why are you beckoning her? How do you know each other?' Thane asked, darkly incredulous.

Augustus straightened to his full height. Thane would give the man points for the gutsy move if he still weren't several inches shorter than him and trying on a smug smirk for size. But what really set Thane's teeth on edge was the way the disturbingly dashing Viscount—who was as suave and golden as Thane was dark and untamed—practically stripped the sheath from Ana's body with his lustful covetous gaze. It made a growl threaten to tear up his throat. He felt as if he could grow fangs.

'Luciana is to be my fiancée, Prince Thane. So I would appreciate it if you...'

The rest of his words were swept away on a tide of realisation and a watery rush sped through his ears, drowning out sound.

'*Fiancée*?' he repeated, black venom oozing from his tone. Because that meant... That meant...

With predator-like grace he pivoted to look back at the woman who had bewitched him so long ago. Invaded his every salacious dream for five years.

Eyes closed, she tucked her lips into her mouth and bit down hard enough to bruise.

'Do I take it I am in the company of Princess Luciana of *Arunthia*?' His voice seethed with distaste, so cold and hard he imagined it could shatter every windowpane within a ten miles radius. '*Am I?*'

His increase in volume snapped her awake and she elevated her chin, stood tall and regal, while she ruthlessly shuttered her expression.

'You certainly are, Prince Thane of *Galancia*,' she said, in a sexy, sassy voice that sent a dark erotic wave of heat rushing down his spine.

Ah, this was his Ana, all right. She looked more fearsome than Augustus could any day of the week, and Thane had the absurd desire to kiss that mulish line right off her lush, sulky mouth. Even *knowing* who she was. A Verbault. Henri's daughter. And didn't *that* fill him with no small amount of self-disgust? This had to be the universe's idea of a sick joke.

Thane crossed his arms over his wide chest and arched one livid brow as they faced off in the hallway.

'Did you know who I was back then?'

Had she known and set out to destroy him by luring him in? Because the Arunthian hussy had almost managed it. Almost driven him to the brink of insanity in the aftermath of her disappearance.

If he'd blinked he would have missed it. The way her smooth throat convulsed. The way she shot a quick glance in Augustus's direction as if to check he was still there. He was. Unfortunately. Soaking up every word.

'I'm afraid I have no idea what you're talking about. I've never met you before in my life. Now, if you gentlemen will excuse me, I suddenly find I'm very tired.'

Stupefied, he rocked back on his heels as she blew past them like a hurricane, leaving her signature trail of destruction in her wake.

A flash fire started in the pit of his gut and his mood took a deadly turn. The voracious heat was exploding to sear through his veins, to fire his blood as pure, undiluted anger blazed through his system.

Had she *actually* denied knowing him? *Him*? Prince Thane of Galancia? Had she *actually* walked away from him? *Again*?

A haze of inky darkness clouded his vision, his mind.

Ah, Princess. Big mistake. *Huge*. Massive, grave error of judgement.

He wanted answers. *Now*. Wanted to know if she'd known his true identity all along. If she'd been toying with him. Why she'd vanished in the middle of the night after she'd promised she would stay. Why she'd plunged him into the pit of Hades for months on end—something he would make her pay dearly for. But most of all he wanted her away from this sleaze-bag. Thane may no longer want to bed her, but he'd be damned if he stood by while Augustus took what was his.

Fact was he wanted her full attention. And, by God, he would get it.

This was not happening. This was just *not* happening.

Luciana shoved her clothes into her suitcase with one hand while she grappled with a cordless phone in the other.

Lord, she was shaking so hard she was likely calling Venezuela. One touch from that man and it was as if she'd been dormant in some cryonic stasis for five years and he'd plugged her into the national grid. Twenty minutes later her body was still burning; incinerator-hot, making her feel like a living, breathing flame.

Dangerous. That was what he was.

Worse still, when she'd literally crashed into him for a split second she'd thought she was dreaming again. That she'd conjured up his memory to save her from the nightmare her return had condemned her to. So often she slept with him in her bed, his fingers a ghost-like touch drifting over her body. Caressing, devouring with a fervour she longed for. And during that breathless moment in that hallway suddenly, shockingly, she'd wanted to cry. Weep in sheer relief that he was here. Holding her once more. Wrapping her in his ferocious unyielding strength.

That body… Such inordinate power that he vibrated with it. She'd met some powerful men in her time but Thane… No comparison. None. His every touch was a jolting shock-wave of acute pleasure and pain. And it had been so long since she'd been touched. She'd almost begged him to crush her against his hard, muscular chest for one blissful second, just so she could live in the illusion that he was here and she was safe.

But that was all it was—a fantasy. A fallacy. She would never be safe in Thane's arms.

So why did a part of her still crave him? Even knowing what and who he was?

Luciana moaned out loud. Her father was right—she was an absolute disgrace.

She'd do well to remember that invariably her dreams turned dark and his hands turned malicious and she woke in a cold, clammy and anguished sweat. That in actuality he was the most lethal, autocratic man in Europe, who co-ruled his country and his people with a merciless iron fist.

And that look in his glorious dark eyes when he'd gazed at her… As if she was his entire world… A lie. Her cruel imagination. If she needed proof to substantiate that theory all she had to do was recall his blistering disgust and anger as he'd ground out her title. Realised her true identity.

His granite-like countenance hadn't broken her heart. Certainly not. The man was rumoured to be a mercenary, for pity's sake.

Imagine that man getting hold of your son and using him as a pawn in his power-play?

Over her dead body.

That hypothesis was akin to someone upending a bucket of cold water over her head and she calmed enough to hit the right keys.

'I need a car outside in five minutes and a private jet waiting at the Altiport to take me to Arunthia. Can you do that?'

'Yes, *madame*.'

'Thank you.'

Depressing the call button, she flipped the lid of her case and yanked the zipper all the way around.

She had to get home. Get Natanael out of the country until she was sure Thane wouldn't come after her. The savage vehemence pouring off him as she'd left had scarred her for eternity. That was *not* a man you messed with.

The tap on her door flung her heart into overdrive and she crept up to the door to peek into the security viewer.

Shoulders slumping, she unlatched the lock and allowed the porter in to collect her bag. 'Thank you. I'll meet you downstairs.' Luciana pulled a two-hundred-euro note from her jacket pocket and conjured up a sweet smile. Feminine wiles and all that.

'The back door, okay?'

His boyish grin told her she was in the clear and she grabbed her handbag and scarpered from the room.

Down in the private elevator she went. Out through the back exit and into a frosty evening that nipped her cheeks.

The door of the limousine was an open invitation and Luciana sank into the plush leather, not wasting one vital moment. 'Can you take me to the Altiport, please? Fast as you can.'

The door slammed shut with a heavy clunk.

The locks clicked into place.

'Sure thing, lady.'

Lady? Frowning, she glanced up into the rearview mirror to see a peculiar pair of deep-set titanium-grey eyes staring back at her.

Luciana's blood curdled in her veins.

Then that voice—as brutal and vicious as the thrash of a whip—sliced through the leather-scented cabin, its deadly effect severing her air supply.

'We meet again, *Princess* of Arunthia.'

Vaulting backwards in her seat, she crushed herself into the corner and scoured the dim recesses of the car, her heart thudding a panicked tempo.

Black sapphire eyes glittering as starkly as the stars in the Courchevel sky, he raised one devilish dark brow and said, scathingly, 'Did you really think I would allow you to turn your back on me a second time, Luciana? Disappear into the night once more? How very foolish of you.'

Dressed from head to foot in a bespoke black Italian suit, he lounged like an insolent predator—a sleek panther perusing his kill.

'Well, let us get one thing perfectly clear right now. *This* time you will *not* walk away from *me*.'

CHAPTER TWO

SHE COULDN'T MOVE. Not one muscle.

'This time you *will* not *walk away from* me.'

What did he mean by that? Did she have to wait until *he* walked away from *her*? How long was that going to take? An hour? A day?

If she didn't start breathing she'd never find out.

Luciana yanked her focus dead ahead in order to stitch up the tattered remnants of her composure. She couldn't do that and look at him at the same time. It was futile. The mere sight of him, dangerous and dominating, skewed her equilibrium and turned her brain to mush.

The privacy glass rose up before her, sending her heart slamming around her ribcage. For a second she toyed with the idea of launching herself from the car, but then remembered the locks had snapped into place. A moment later the limousine began to rock down the steep incline from the lodge and the risk of hyperventilating became a distinct possibility.

Breathe, Luce, for heaven's sake breathe. He probably just wants to talk on the way to the Altiport.

Why, oh, why hadn't she looked at which car she was getting into? She was supposed to be avoiding trouble. Being good. The refined, beyond reproach, virtuous Queen she was born to be. She could already hear her mother... *So reckless, Luciana. So unthinking.*

She let loose a shaky exhalation, then took a deep lungful

of air. And another. Then seriously wished she hadn't. His audacious dark bergamot and amber scent wrapped around her senses like a narcotic, intensely potent and drugging as it swirled up into her brain, making her vision blur. Her entire body wept with want.

How did he still do this to her? After all this time? *How*? It was as if he engulfed her in his power, lured her in with his black magic. Well, any more of his lethal brand of masculinity and she'd be done for.

Clearing her throat, she straightened in her seat. With far more sangfroid and bravado than she felt, she said, 'Why am I here? What *exactly* is it you want from me?'

Seconds ticked by and he didn't so much as murmur. Merely allowed the atmosphere to stretch taut. And, since she was hanging on to the very last fraying threads of her control, it didn't take her long to snap.

Up came her head—*big* mistake as she realised too late it was exactly what he'd been waiting for, what he wanted: her full attention, total control over this…whatever *this* was. His gaze crashed into hers. Unerringly. Mercilessly.

Oh, Lord.

Overwhelming anguish held her in stasis as her every thought fled and she allowed her treacherous heart to devour the dark beauty that was Prince Thane.

Devastating—that was what he was. Bewitching her with that breathtaking aura of danger. Those high, wide slashing cheekbones and obsidian eyes framed with thick decadent inky lashes. That chiselled jaw that was smothered in a seriously sexy short beard. On anyone else it would be labelled designer stubble. But this was Thane and he wasn't vain in the least. Or he hadn't been. In truth, she'd been amazed at just how clueless to his gorgeous looks he was.

His hair was longer, she noticed. *Dishevelled* was a ridiculously romantic word for the mussed-up glossy black hair that fell in a tumble to flick his shoulders, one side swept back and tucked behind his ear. Unkempt, maybe.

Hideously long… But she kind of liked it. Craved to run her fingers through it. Had to fist her hands to stop herself from doing just that.

The dim interior lighting camouflaged his facial scars but she remembered every one. The slash in his top lip, just shy of the full cupid's bow. The second, enhancing the sensuous, kissable divot in his chin. Another slicing into the outer corner of his left eyebrow.

Her throat grew tight, swelling in sadness and hurt for him. Just as it had five years ago. Not that he'd ever talked to her about them. The one time she'd asked he'd shut down so hard it had taken her sitting astride his lap wearing nothing but lace panties to tease him out of it.

Ah, Luce, don't remember. Don't.

His tongue sneaked out and he briefly licked his lips, but otherwise he remained still, watching…waiting…his sensationally dynamic body vibrating with dark power. And she clutched her handbag tighter still, fingers burying into the leather—

Whether it was the feel of her phone poking through the side of her bag or the sudden realisation that the car was at a standstill she wasn't sure, but she crashed back to earth with a thud.

The car had actually stopped!

Luciana shuffled on her bottom to peek out of the window and saw the huge security gates of the lodge swing open in front of the car. Electronic operation. Unmanned. Drat.

Twisting the other way, she grasped the cushioned leather and peeked out of the back window, her eyes widening as she spied her bellboy, still at the top of the drive, waving for her attention, with her case in his hand.

Oh, my life!

Her speech faculties finally deigned to kick in. 'You have to turn around,' she said, with her best do-it-or-else regal intonation. 'You've left my case back there.'

And as soon as they pulled up back at the lodge she was making a run for it.

'Really?' he drawled, mock astonishment lifting his brows high above his vivid eyes. 'How unfortunate.'

Luciana narrowed her gaze on him. That was it? *Unfortunate?*

'Well? Aren't you going to go back for it?' she asked, her tone pitched to an ear-splitting squeak.

'And give you the opportunity to run again? I think not, *princesa*. Consider yourself under lock and key.'

The limo turned right onto the main road and picked up speed. But not nearly as fast as her temper.

Anger sparked. Revving up to be free of its leash. And she let it take hold. Uncoil deep inside her. Unravel at a breakneck pace. It was wonderful. Glorious. Just what she'd hankered for all day. *All day?* No. Since she'd stepped off the plane from Hong Kong, thoroughly powerless, with her façade firmly in place.

'Just *who* do you think you are? You can't just *take* me like this.'

Cool as you like, he simply said, 'Watch me.'

She sucked in air through her nose. 'Are you playing with me? You're taking me to the Altiport, right? I have a plane to catch.'

'We *are* going to the Altiport, *si*.'

'Good. That's good.'

Though he hadn't really said what was happening when they got there, had he?

Warily, she ventured, 'And you'll let me get on my own plane to Arunthia, yes?'

'No.'

Mouth falling agape, she coughed out an incredulous laugh. 'Are you *serious*?'

'Deadly,' he said, as sharp as a blade.

His eyes were as cold and hard as steel. Where once they'd been tender and warm. Had she known him at all?

she wondered, fighting a miserable flare of anguish. Even a little bit? Or had the last few years killed any ounce of decency and compassion he'd possessed?

Icy fingers of dread curled around her throat. 'So where *are* you taking me?'

'Galancia.'

The world tilted as if the car had skidded down an embankment with a five-score gradient and she went woozy. *Galancia?* No, no, *no*!

Luciana scoured his expression, desperate to find even a flicker of his dry humour, and came up blank. Galancia… She shuddered in her own skin.

'No way. You haven't got a hope in hell of getting me to that place. I have to go home.'

He pursed his lips and cocked his head in faux contemplation. 'Not today. Today you will go where I ordain.'

'But…but that's tantamount to abduction!'

'I suppose technically it is. Yet during the several minutes we've been in this car I haven't heard you call for assistance once.'

It didn't bode well that he was right. But, honest to God, the man was so distracting. Still, why *wasn't* she petrified out of her mind, screeching her head off?

'Give me a second and I'll scream blue murder. Though let's face it,' she said, gesturing to the luxurious car. 'There's no one to hear me, is there?'

'Not now, no. You are seven minutes too late, *princesa*. Though Seve may help you.'

'Who on earth is Seve?'

'The driver.'

She almost shuffled to the edge of the bench seat and raised her fist to knock on the glass partition. Almost. Frankly, she knew better.

'Friend?'

'Cousin,' he drawled, a flicker of a devilish smile playing about his mouth.

It was obscene how relieved she was to see that tiny flirtation with humour—that hint of the man she'd fallen for on a raucous, cluttered muddy field in Zurich. Particularly since it suggested he was enjoying her discomfort. What was all this? Payback for her walking away? Some kind of twisted revenge?

'You can't go about kidnapping people. It isn't civilised behaviour.'

Lord, she sounded like her mother. And, honestly, only a dimwit would put 'civilised' and 'Thane' in the same sentence. It had been his untamed earthy savagery that had attracted her in the first place. Obviously she had a screw loose.

Blasé, he gave her an insouciant shrug that said, *try and stop me*, and it made her anger boil into lava-hot fury until she felt like a mini-volcano on the verge of eruption. What *was* it about men trying to govern her life? She'd just escaped one control freak and run headlong into another.

Smouldering with resentment, she decided she wanted him to erupt too. It was as if he'd switched off his emotions. He was far too cool and collected over there. While she was sitting here losing it!

Look at him, she thought. Sitting at an angle, one leg bent and resting on the bench seat, he sprawled like a debauched lion, taking over half the enormous car—and *all* of the oxygen—in that outrageously expensive Italian suit. It *should* have oozed elegance and debonair refinement, but it made him look like pure wickedness and carnal sin.

And she detested him for making her hormones whisk themselves into a deranged frenzy over him. Wasn't she in enough of a mess?

Which reminded her... Woman on a mission, here. She wanted the playing field levelled.

'So the rumours are true, then?' she said, with as much chilly, haughty daring as she could muster.

Thane arched one arrogant brow. 'There are so many I'm at a loss as to which particular falsehood you refer to.'

'That your men steal women. That your father took your mother from her bed—stole her from her intended.' And by all accounts made her life a living hell in Galancia Castle. Rumour had it she'd thrown herself to her death to end the torment. Not that Luciana had ever believed that bit. No mother would do that to her son, surely?

Luciana waited him out. Expecting some kind of reaction. Something. *Anything.* What she got frustrated her even more. Nothing. Not even a flutter of his ridiculously gorgeous lashes.

'Ah, that one. Perfectly true. Indeed, we take what is rightfully ours.'

She was going to slap him in a second. 'And *where*, pray tell, do you get the idea that *I* am rightfully yours?'

Aha! As if she'd flipped a switch emotion stormed through his eyes. The dark variety. But right now she'd take what she could get.

'What is *rightfully* mine, Luciana, is an explanation. Answers.'

'That's all you want from me. An explanation?' It seemed a bit too easy to her, but she could answer fifty questions before they got anywhere near a plane. It was a thirty-minute drive at least. 'Fine,' she bit out. 'Ask away, Prince Thane. What do you want to know? Why I bolted in the dead of night?'

'Ah…' he said, with an affable lilt that belied the fury now emanating from him. 'So you *do* acknowledge that we have a history. Yet not thirty minutes ago you denied we'd ever met.'

Blast her runaway mouth. She should have known that would antagonise him.

'Yes, well, I don't want Augustus knowing about my personal life.'

'Worried, Luciana? That the prissy Viscount will not wish

to bed you or wed you any longer when he discovers you've been tarnished by our depraved association?'

She huffed. 'Hardly.' That would only be a *good* thing. And, absurd as it was, she suddenly had the strangest compulsion to thank her kidnapper for rescuing her from tonight's unpalatable proposal. Clearly she'd lost the plot.

As for his darkly intoned question—she'd lied through her teeth because all she cared about was making sure Augustus never put two and two together if he was ever faced with Natanael.

Natanael… *Oh, Lord.* She'd wanted to text him before he went to sleep. But it was far too risky to fish her phone from her handbag right now. The bag she clutched to her stomach like a lifeline. Thank goodness she'd carried it and not left it with her case.

More to the point, thank heavens she hadn't brought Nate to the Alps with her. The thought of Thane discovering him…carting him off to Galancia… No, that could never happen. *Never.* Thane was descended from a long line of militia. Royal males trained in guerrilla warfare. The best fighter pilots in the world. Some said all the boys were taken to the barracks to learn how to become soldiers at eight years old. The mere thought of Nate holding a weapon in four years' time made acid rise and coat her throat. Plus, she really had no idea what Thane was capable of. Considering abduction was his modus operandi for their reunion.

She shuddered where she sat, swelling until she felt she might burst with the need to protect Nate at all costs. She hadn't kept his identity a secret all this time to lose him now. Her little boy was having a long, happy and healthy life even if it killed her.

At this rate, Luce, it just might.

When she realised Thane was speaking again, she turned to face him and watched the soft skin around his eyes crinkle as he narrowed those black sapphire peepers on her.

'So you do not care? You do not care that your *fiancé* may no longer want you—?'

'He is *not* my fiancé.' Not yet anyway. And she'd rather bask in the fantasy of freedom a while longer, thank you very much.

'Now, are you *sure* about that, Luciana?' he jeered. 'Because he seemed to think you are. Or is your word now as empty as it was five years ago?'

She made a tiny choked squeak of affront. 'And what exactly do you mean by that?'

Brooding and fierce, he leaned forward, attacking her brain with another infusion of his darkly sensual scent. 'You made a promise to me. That you'd stay another week. That we would talk.'

She could virtually feel how tightly reined in he was, and Luciana delved into his turbulent stormy eyes because...was that *hurt* in his voice? Surely not. How could *she* possibly hurt this man? No. If anything she'd bruised his male ego. A man who wielded his kind of power likely wasn't accustomed to being deserted.

Though either way, to be fair, she *had* promised him she would stay. Hadn't she?

Yes. She had. They'd become hot and heavy so fast she'd wanted to tell him who she really was. Not to have lies whispering between the damp, tangled sheets. Because in her mind there'd been something so beautiful and pure about what they'd had together the dishonesty had shredded her heart.

She swallowed around the great lump in her throat. It was torture to remember. Utter torture. 'I did promise you—you're right. But that was before I found out who you were.'

With his bent elbow resting on the lip of the window, he curled his index finger over his mouth pensively and stared at her. 'So you didn't know who I was all along?'

Mouth arid, she licked over her lips. 'No, I didn't know who you were. Of course I didn't.'

'Are you telling me the truth? You swear it?'

'Yes.' Did he think she'd duped him? 'I couldn't have set up the way we met even if I tried, Thane. Don't you remem—?'

Slam! She locked the vault shut before all the memories it had taken her so long to ensnare were unleashed. Escaping to create havoc in her soul. Best to forget. For all their sakes.

'Let's just call it an ironic twist of fate,' she said, hearing the melancholy in her voice. 'We were young. Stupid. Reckless. I didn't know you at all. I'd fallen into bed with a stranger…' *And I awoke to a nightmare.* 'I found your papers, Thane.'

She'd never forget that moment as long as she lived. Standing in the dim light of their bathroom, feeling naked and exposed, his nationality papers for travel that she'd stumbled across quivering in her hand. The realisation she was sleeping with the enemy.

'And after three, almost four weeks,' he said fiercely, 'of our being inseparable, spending every waking and sleeping moment together, your first instinct was to run? With not *one* word? Do you have *any* idea…?'

Veering away from her, he clenched his jaw so tight she heard his molars groan in protest. And she swiftly reassessed the idea that she'd caused him pain by leaving the way she had.

Remorse gathered in the space behind her ribs and trickled down into her stomach to merge with the ever-present pool of guilt that swelled and churned with her secrets every minute of every day. The painful struggle between truth and darkness.

But, looking back, she remembered she'd been consumed with the need to flee.

First had come denial and bewilderment. She'd been unable to match the dark, dangerous, merciless Prince with the somewhat shy—at least around women—rock music lover who'd held her cherishingly tight through endless nights of bliss. Then terror had set in, leaving her panic-stricken, contemplating how he'd react when he discovered who she was. And heartache, knowing she had to leave before he found out. Knowing that while she toyed with the temptation of staying in touch, meeting up again, suddenly another hour was too much of a hazard, a risk, never mind some far-off midnight tryst.

So she'd run. Taken the good memories instead of tainting them with bitterness and regret. Run as fast as she could with her heart tearing apart.

Glancing out at the snow-capped peaks of the Tarentaise Valley, she took a deep breath and then exhaled, her warm breath painting a misty cloud upon the window. If he needed closure in order to forget and let her go, then so be it.

'I'm sorry I didn't let you know I was leaving. Write you a note or something. I didn't mean to hurt you that way. But it was over. We had an affair—that's all. There could never have been a future for us.'

Chills skittered over her skin and she crossed her arms over her chest, rubbing the gooseflesh from her shoulders. She was so lost in thought she didn't notice his hand reaching across the back of the bench seat until it was in her periphery and she flinched. Hard. Unsure what to expect from him.

'Are you afraid of me now?' he asked, his voice gruff as if she'd sanded the edge off his volatility.

Was she afraid of him? Genuinely?

No. Though she couldn't really understand why.

Because deep down you know he won't hurt you. Deep down you know the man who took your innocence with such gentle passionate persuasion would never physically hurt you in a million years.

But that didn't mean he couldn't emotionally destroy her. And Nate. *That* he was capable of.

So maybe she *did* fear him. Just not in the way he meant.

Luciana gave her head a little shake and he picked up a lock of her hair and rubbed the strands between his fingertips. 'I wouldn't have recognised you. How different you look this way.'

She had the ludicrous desire to ask him if he liked the way she looked. The real her. Or if he'd fallen for a black-haired hippy who didn't exist. But the reality was it was best she didn't know.

'It was a lifetime ago,' she said, immensely proud of her strong voice when she felt so weak when he was close. 'Forget the person I pretended to be in Zurich. I was just...' She had to swallow hard to push the words out. 'Acting out. Letting loose. Having a bit of fun.'

Such a lie. But maybe if he thought their wild, hedonistic fling meant nothing to her he'd hate her. Let her go...

Et voilà.

Easing back, he created a distance that felt as deep and wide as the Arunthian falls.

'Fun,' he repeated tonelessly. 'Well, that makes both of us.'

Her stomach plunged to the leather seat with a disheartened thump. Because it was just as she'd always suspected.

Stiffening her spine, she brushed her hair back from her face. 'There you go, then. There really is no point in dragging this out.'

He said nothing. Simply leaned back and glared at her with such intensity she felt transparent.

Jittery, she shifted in her seat and rammed her point home.

'Thane, you have to let me go back to Arunthia. To my family. They need me. I've got to get married soon. I—'

'No.'

'*No*? But haven't I given you an explanation? What more could you possibly want from me?'

'That is a very good question, *princesa*.'

And Luciana had the feeling she wasn't going to like the answer. Not one bit.

CHAPTER THREE

THANE IGNORED THE eyes that were boring into his skull and riffled through the mini-bar of the limousine for some hard liquor. She was turning him to drink already—he was insane even to contemplate what enticed his mind.

Snatching a miniature of bourbon, he unscrewed the lid, then tipped the contents onto his tongue and let the fiery liquid trickle down his throat in a heavenly slow burn.

From the corner of his eye he saw Luciana pick up a bottle of sparkling water and commanded himself not to look, to watch. To devour all that beautiful, riveting bone structure—her nose a delicate slope of pure femininity, pronounced razor-sharp cheekbones a supermodel would kill for—those intoxicating brandy-gold eyes and that glossy, over-full wanton mouth as she drank.

Dios, she made his flesh and blood blaze. And it had been so long since he'd felt anything that he was consumed. By want. By hate. It was a terrifically violent and lethal combination that was taking all of his will power to control.

While she speared darts of ire or disbelief in his direction, poised and elegant in her glamorous couture black and white ensemble, all *he* could think of was her pupils dilated, her hair tossed over his pillow in gloriously messy abandon, and raw, primal sheet-clawing passion.

But it was more than that, wasn't it? He'd thought his memories were long dead, murdered by the passage of time and the strife in Galancia, but since he'd touched her he'd started to remember.

Remember being held close against her bare skin, feeling truly wanted—a real man made from flesh and hot blood, willing to pay whatever price it took to sustain that feeling a while longer. And, while he wanted that back, he knew it was lost to him.

'Having a bit of fun. Letting loose.'

Any molecule of hope he'd harboured that she'd felt something for him disintegrated, and inside his chest that lump of stone where his heart should be cracked down the centre and crumbled to dust.

Good. He didn't want the weak and tender emotions involved in this. Never had to begin with. But the beguiling creature had lured him in. Lesson learned.

'Are you going to tell me what's going on in that head of yours?' she asked, before gnawing on her crimson bruised bottom lip.

'As soon as I figure it out, yes.' Because despite his misgivings, despite what she'd said, something…*something* told him she held the key to his fate. He couldn't explain it if he tried—just as he'd never been able to explain how he'd known she was in grave danger the day they'd met. How when their eyes had locked he'd known she belonged to him.

Ignorant of his internal debate, she heaved a great sigh at his cool reply. But it had taken him less than ten seconds to figure out the best way to play this game: total emotional lockdown. Which was no inconsiderable feat when that aloof haughtiness kept invading her body like some freakish poltergeist and he was overcome with the violent need to grab her and shake it loose. Then there was the way her mind clearly often wandered down a path that he suspected was paved with turmoil, because guilt would walk all over her face. It made him want to climb into her brain and seduce her secrets.

The bright lights of the Altiport runway came into view,

as did his sleek black private jet embellished with the Guerrero family crest—a large snake curling around the blade of a sword—and she clutched her bag to her chest as if it held the crown jewels. Which, he conceded, might be true. His knowledge of women's paraphernalia was zilch.

'Thane, look. Be reasonable about this. I'm your enemy—there isn't anything I could give you but trouble. For starters, the bellboy saw me drive away in your car. Does he know who you are?'

He shrugged his wide shoulders. 'I imagine so. I believe I am very difficult to miss.'

She rolled her eyes. 'Arrogance really should be your middle name. My point is: come morning, Augustus will know I'm with you. Then he'll call my father—because, let me tell you, they are as thick as thieves. Soon after my father will be on the warpath. So you *have* to let me go home. My family will worry if I just vanish into thin air.'

'Let them suffer,' he said. Just as *he'd* done. Trying to fill the empty, aching void of losing her. Had she cared for him? Obviously not.

She huffed in disgust. 'Well, how gallant of you. How would *you* feel if someone you loved disappeared off the face of the earth?'

His mouth shaped to tell her he knew exactly how it felt, but first his pride stopped him, and then her words. *Love?* This had nothing to do with love. He was a protective man by nature, and naturally that extended to her. She'd been his. Correction: she *was* his. Regardless of her true identity. Moreover, he would kiss Arunthian soil before he admitted any hint of vulnerability to *her*. To anyone. He'd been nine years old when he'd last made that mistake—telling his father that enclosed spaces made him violently sick. Twenty-four hours down an abandoned well had taught him much.

'Honestly, could you be a more heartless brute?'

It didn't escape him that he'd been called worse things in

his time—a murderer, a mercenary, a traitor—so why the devil it stung coming from her was a mystery.

'I'm sure I could if I put my mind to it,' he drawled darkly.

'But you're going to be a wanted man. Do you want to spend the rest of your days in a jail cell?'

Thane turned to face her and raised one mocking eyebrow. 'Your father would have to catch me first *princesa*— and, believe me, *that* is impossible.'

'It's not about catching *you*,' she said, pointing at his shirt before turning the same finger back on herself. 'He'll come for *me*. Do you want an Arunthian army on your doorstep?'

As if.

'They would never get through Galancian airspace. Do you forget who I am? Your security and your army are no match for mine.'

'You're probably right. But that's because we are peace-keepers. Not fighters. Our people don't live in fear of an iron-fisted rule. We are rich in life and happiness and that is more important to us.'

Thane scoffed. Did she think he didn't want those things for his own people? What did she think he fought for? The good of his health? But the topic did bring him full circle to his hellishly risky concept. She could, in effect, help him gain a better life for them. Relax that iron-fisted rule she'd just accused him of by placing his crown in his hands.

Dios, it was mad even to think any union could possibly work, but the notion spun his brain into a frenzied furore. Snagging on one name: Augustus.

He was the biggest unknown in all of this. What the hell was a woman like Luciana doing with a scumbag like him? He was missing something vital here, and he did not appreciate having only half the intel on a situation.

During the twenty minutes he'd waited for her to emerge from the lodge he'd accessed every file he could uncover.

Princess Luciana Valentia Thyssen Verbault. Born and raised in Arunthia. Schooled at Eton and Cambridge, England. No record of her time in Zurich. No surprise there, since she'd been a carousing black-haired gypsy. Five years in China. Low-key. There was only the odd photograph during that time, either with a dark-haired friend and two small boys, or back home at a royal function—as if she'd returned to Arunthia for that purpose entirely, only to travel straight back to China. So what had been there to lure her back again and again? A job? Maybe. But why did his instincts tell him it was a man?

One thing was clear: unless he got a better picture of her life his plans would be dead in the water before he'd even launched them off the jetty.

While all this circled around in his head like manic vultures, Luciana launched into another talkfest about Arunthia: how content the people were, how he could learn a thing or two. The bare-faced cheek of it! Her arms wafted in the air as she warmed to her subject. And, *Dios*, no matter what crap came out of her mouth, she was the picture of enthralling passionate beauty.

He'd adored that about her. How she could talk for hours. About nothing in particular. Silly, mundane things—music, movies and architecture. He'd revelled in that freedom from his responsibilities, the chance to forget the trouble at home for a while. Ironic that he'd chosen a Zurich festival, having been once before in his uni days, to get away from it all and met a woman from his own sphere who'd been doing exactly the same thing.

An odd memory hit and a smile curved his lips. One she caught.

'What?'

'I was just thinking of the time we went to the cinema and were thrown out because you wouldn't stop talking.'

A lie.

'Talking? We didn't get thrown out because we were *talking*. We got evicted because we were…' Heat plumed in the rapidly shrinking confines of the car, driving a flush high across her cheekbones. 'Never mind.'

He felt so smug he could hear his own grin. 'Shall I finish that for you?'

'No, thank you. It's best if we don't go there, okay?'

She was right. He should be getting a handle on her relationship with the Viscount, not testing her memory. Not watching that beautiful blush frisk down her neck and caress her collarbone. Not inhaling her subtle vanilla and jasmine scent until his body prickled with heat and unleashed a firestorm of memories that turned him hard as steel.

Like the sensation of those plump lips softening beneath his as she'd surrendered to him. The way she'd felt when he'd thrust inside her virginal tight body. The way her legs had curled around his waist as he took her over and over. Lithe, svelte legs…glossed with skin that had felt like finely powdered icing sugar beneath his palms and tasted just as sweet. The softest, most exquisite texture he'd ever touched. Legs that were taunting him now because they were fuller. Lusher. Just like her breasts…

Thane shifted in his seat, the creak of leather sharpening his arousal as his body roared to life. Feral lust pushed incessantly against his zipper. Worse still, she exacerbated his darkly erotic state by squirming and lifting her hair from her nape as if she were over-hot. Well, that made two of them.

Depressing the window button, he let the cool air slither through the gap in a wispy sheet of fog and relished the odd snowflake that settled on the back of his hand.

Luciana's answer was to snatch a bar of chocolate from the mini-bar and have ravenous sex with every bite. He could virtually hear her silent moans.

'Hungry?' he asked, his voice as thick as his throat.

She licked the sweet treat from her lips with a sensual flick of her tongue. 'Erm…yes. Dinner was awful.'

He took the opening for what it was. Perfect for getting him back on track. 'The food or the company?'

Her gaze drifted to stare unseeingly out of the tinted window. The runway floodlights flickered over her at intervals, highlighting the honeycomb strands in her lavish hair and lending her skin an incandescent glow.

Ethereal was surely the only word to describe her in that moment. Seraphic. And his ardour dulled as he was struck with the feeling that he was too dark to touch her. That he would taint her somehow.

Right at this moment she was crushed up against the door, as far away from him as she could get, and Thane hardened his body, trying to expunge the terrible self-awareness, the stomach ache that whispered of rejection. Not once had she rebuffed their volatile passion. Not once. The reason for which he wanted to know. *Now.*

'You never answered my question,' he said, his tone darkly savage. 'Was it the food or the company that was so bad you could not eat?'

Her absurdly long, decadent eyelashes were downswept. 'Does it matter?' she asked softly.

Patience dwindling, he went in for the kill. Even though he was unsure if he could go through with this if she said yes.

Astounding and unthinkable as it was, if she did he'd rather put her on an Arunthian plane without another word. The 'why' of it wouldn't be difficult to find if he cared to revisit his boyhood, watch misery trickle down his mother's face as she pined for another. But delve into the past he would not. That long-ago place was a dark punishment he would never descend to again.

'Are you in love with Augustus, Luciana?'

She massaged her temple as if he were a headache she wished to rub away.

'I wasn't born to marry for love, Thane. I have no choice over the direction my life takes.' Her voice was tinged with bitterness and he felt a flicker of suspicion spark in his gut.

Frowning, he narrowed his eyes on her face, his guts twisting into a noxious tangle. 'Have you been in his bed?'

If he'd blinked he would have missed it. Her wince of distaste.

'That is none of your business.'

'Have you been in his bed, Luciana?' he asked again—harder, darker. Almost cutthroat.

'What difference does it make?'

'For hell's sake, just answer the question!'

Up came her arms with an exasperated toss. '*No!* Okay? I haven't been anywhere near his rotten bed. Would *you* want to?' She groaned aloud as if she wished the words back, and shoved another chunk of chocolate between her pink lips.

Thane felt a smile kick the corner of his mouth as relief doused over him like a warm shower of summer rain. That temper of hers still gave her a candid, somewhat strident bent.

'And you still intend to *marry* this man?' Even though the idea appalled her?

'Yes.'

He would have to be six feet under first.

Clearly Henri was pushing her into it. *That bastard.* He should have killed the man years ago, when he'd had the chance. Fury pummelled at him to think she was being forced to the altar as his mother had been. And Thane's every protective instinct kicked in—he wanted her kept far away from Henri and Augustus. Where neither of them could reach her.

'You will not touch him, *comprende*? Nor will you allow him to touch you.'

Not that he was giving her the chance to do either.

Huffing a little, she arched one fair brow. 'That's going to prove a bit difficult when we are married, Thane.'

'Which is precisely the reason you are not marrying him.'

His mind was set. Firstly, she had the rarity of blue blood, and a union with her would give him his crown. Four years early. His struggles to build a better life for his people would end. His uncle's dictatorship would cease as Thane took total control of the throne. Finally he could make amends.

And secondly—he easily silenced the impish taunt of his earlier words—there would be no riding bareback into hell as he aligned with the enemy. Because while she might be a Verbault at this moment, Thane would soon make her a Guerrero. Tomorrow seemed as good a day as any. Saving her from a fate worse than death—namely the vapid Viscount and her father's political clutches.

Win-win. Let it not be said that he wasn't knight in shining armour material.

A faint crease lined her forehead as she fingered back the curtain of her hair to glance at him warily. 'I…I'm not?'

This could go two ways, he decided. Either he'd be flooded with a profusion of gratitude or she'd fight him under the influence of some misplaced loyalty to her father. So it was a good job there wasn't a battle he couldn't win.

'No. Instead you are marrying me.'

CHAPTER FOUR

IN THE DISTANCE Luciana heard the driver's door open, then close with a deft clunk. Then came a cacophony of voices that fluttered around the car—the cadence low, masculine. And all the while she stared at Thane, who wore a mask of impermeable steel. Her mouth was working but no sound was emerging as she swung like a pendulum, lurching from fighting tears of frustration to biting back a laugh that was sure to lean over to the hysterical side—because the proposal she'd expected had finally come to pass. From the wrong man entirely.

Are you sure about that, Luce?

Yes, she was sure—of course she was sure.

And the worst thing about all of this…? For a split second all she'd seen was Thane and all she'd heard was 'marry' and 'me', and the little girl inside her who'd gorged on fairytales and dreams of love—the one who *hadn't* seen the darker side of marriage and was blissfully unaware of her duties—had felt her heart leap to her throat in utter joy.

Foolish little girl. Foolish heart.

Blame it on temple-pounding awkwardness, but the silence finally pressed a sound from her throat.

'Thane? Are you crazy?'

Crazy? He was insane. Mad as a hatter. Nutty as a goddamn fruitcake.

'Quite probably.'

There, you see—he's even admitted it.

'We're enemies, or have you conveniently forgotten that?'

Oh, she could just imagine Thane having a chinwag with her father. *Hey, do you remember me? The one who tried to assassinate you? Well, I want to marry your daughter.* Yeah, that would go down well. *Not.*

If he *had* attempted the assassination. But why would her father spout such a heinous lie? Truth was, she was drowning in reasons why she couldn't marry him. And that was without broaching the topic of Natanael.

'You and I are not enemies, Luciana.'

His eyes took on the lustrous glitter of the black sapphires they reminded her of and she shivered in response.

'Any chance of that ended when I took your innocence five years ago and made you mine. If your father and my uncle wish to prolong the feud that's up to them, but it has no bearing on our future.'

She shook her head in disbelief. Bad idea. Dizziness took the car, and her, for a little spin. 'How can you say that?'

'Easily. I am my own man, and I will not be dictated to by anyone or anything.'

A scoff burst past her lips. 'Bully for you. I, however, don't have a choice.'

'Which is precisely why I am giving you an alternative.'

So it would seem. The question was: why? He wanted her away from Augustus—that much was evident. Every time the other man's name was brought up he visibly fumed, until she half expected him to snort fire like some great mystical dragon. As if the thought of the other man touching her was abhorrent to him. But not because he loved her. No, no. His biting words from earlier were enough of a clue… *'We take what is rightfully ours. I made you mine…'*

So in effect she could be a Picasso he'd spotted at Christie's and fancied would look wonderful mounted above his machete rack. A beautiful possession.

Fire-tipped arrows pierced her chest and flamed up her throat.

'Well, thank you for the offer,' she said satirically. 'But I'm not keen on your alternative, Thane. For starters, it's simply another demand. And, let me tell you, they are certainly racking up this month.' Her insides were shaking so hard it made her voice quiver. 'And another thing: unfortunately for you, as far as courting rituals and practices go, abduction does *not* score points.'

He frowned deeply and looked at the magazine pouch. As if he was spectacularly disorientated and the answer to her meltdown lay between the covers of the latest gossip rag.

Idly scratching his sexy, stubbled jaw, he glanced back up. 'Courting?'

Luciana blinked. Out of that entire speech, 'courting' was what he'd picked up on? 'Yes, Thane. Dating, courting.'

Surely he couldn't still be as mystified about women as he'd been five years ago? He must have had a truckload since then; he was sex incarnate. Not that she cared what he did. Absolutely not.

'You would prefer this?' he asked, stunned but apparently game.

Luciana squeezed her eyes shut. Lord, this was utterly surreal.

'My father would never give his blessing in a billion years.' Hypothetically speaking, of course. Frankly, she had no idea why she was engaging in this conversation. It was all impossible.

'I care not,' he drawled, his arrogance and power so potent she could taste it. 'If the man wants a fight on his hands for you he can have it. Gladly. He obviously cares little for you to subject you to such a marriage.'

Luciana eased back, pulling her spine upright. She rewound that little speech of his and replayed it in her head. Then felt butterflies take flight in her chest—winged creatures flapping furiously against her ribcage. Had he just said he would fight for her? She was pretty sure he had. As well as intimating that he cared for her happiness. Sort of.

Her thumb found its way to her mouth and she nibbled on the soft pad.

This was the behaviour of a callous mercenary? *Really?* No, of course it wasn't—she must be missing something. He had to have an agenda. Other than his ridiculous chest-thumping caveman routine, that was.

Problem was, when he fixated on the way she sucked her thumb, with wicked heat smouldering in his dark eyes, she couldn't think what day it was—never mind decipher his ulterior motives.

Maybe he wants you for you. Maybe your father was wrong about him. Maybe his reputation isn't as bad as it seems.

Luciana shook her head vehemently. No. That would mean she'd run when she shouldn't have. Made a mistake. And she refused to believe that. After all, proof of his piti-less, ruthless nature wasn't hard to descry, was it? Look where she was, for heaven's sake—atop the highest asphalted runway in Europe, about to be manhandled onto a plane!

On the verge of a panic attack, or at the very least an undignified fainting spell, she yanked at the door handle and—*yes!*—it gave way under the pressure of her grip and she flung it wide.

A second later she launched herself from the car, almost breaking her neck as her heels hit a dusty sheet of new-fallen snow and she slipped…swayed…then skidded to a stop.

Adrenaline spiked her pulse and she glanced left and right, back and forth, wildly searching for a way out. Even as her legs turned to lead at the very thought.

Stupid legs. Stupid heart.

Inhaling swift and deep, she slowly refocused her vi-sion on the mountainous white peaks looming from all an-gles. Dangerous. Breathtaking. Much like the man who now strode around the back of the limousine, moving towards her with a warrior's effortless grace. And yet she felt every step like a seismic rumble.

Instinctively she staggered backwards and pushed out her hand in a stop sign. 'Don't come any closer!'

Snow drizzled from the sky in fat, puffy white flakes and swirled around his tall, commanding body in eddies and whirls as if drawn to his magnetism. The braver ones dared to touch, settle on his ebony hair, kiss his broad shoulders, tease the lapels of his jacket—only to be annihilated in an instant by his unfathomable heat.

Stupid snowflakes.

'Luciana. Don't fight me,' he cajoled, in that sinful voice that made her shudder.

Translation—*Roll over and take it. Be a good girl and do as you're told.*

Yeah, right.

His hands fisted before he stretched the kinks from his fingers and lifted them to spear into his hair; brushing the damp glossy strands back from his forehead, bringing his face into sharp relief.

Oh, Lord.

Her insides panged on a swift stab of anguish. Natanael… The resemblance was spooky. Surreal. Bittersweet and oddly wonderful at the same time.

Arms plunging to his sides, he tipped his head and gave her a crooked smile. 'We need to leave. Come with me.'

Fighting the sting at the back of her eyes, she wrapped her arms around herself, hugging her body. 'No. I can't go with you, Thane. I'm sorry. And I can't marry you. I have to take my throne in two months. I have responsibilities of my own.'

But more than that—much more—I have a son at home: one you can never find, because I'm frightened of what will become of him. I have to protect him. You keep confusing me and I can't trust my instincts with you.

Fact was, she had no idea who this man truly was.

So find out, Luce. Go with him. Find out.

It was a risk she couldn't possibly take. Something told her that if she left with him she'd never return home. Thane would never let her go. His formidable dominance would wrap her up tighter than any other person ever could. Including her father. Loath as she was to admit it, at least if she married Augustus Nate would be safe—and so would she. Her emotions would never engage with *him*.

All that swarthy, sexy maleness took on a blistering intensity as Thane dipped his chin and locked his fierce gaze on her.

'That throne will not be yours if you marry that man, Luciana. You know it. And maybe your responsibilities now lie with me.'

Temper igniting inside her, she balled her fists. 'No, they *really* don't.'

He hitched one shoulder, as if to say he wasn't going to argue about it, that she should just take his word and accept it. Talk about *déjà vu*. It was like standing in front of her father's desk, listening to the latest of his twenty commandments.

And that was it. It dawned on her that there was just no point in arguing. None.

From the corner of her eye she noticed a workman bundled in ski gear as he fought the elements, dragging safety cones across the asphalt, and knew exactly what she had to do.

Luciana took one last look at Thane's dark beauty and memorised every wicked, gorgeous inch of him. Then she hiked her chin and declared, 'I am *not* getting on that plane with you. Goodbye, Thane.'

Off she went, veering in the workman's direction, begging her feet not to slip. Cursing herself for not taking three extra minutes back at the lodge to change her clothes.

'Excuse me?' she called out. 'Hello? Helloooo…?'

His head came up, eyes latched onto her and he waved back.

Thank the heavens above.

Keep walking, Luce, just keep walking—

'Oh, no, you don't.'

An ironclad hand curled around her upper arm and next thing she knew she'd collided with Thane's hot, hard, magnificent body.

Fear and excitement shot through her in equal measure. Yet her protest went the way of her sanity when he pulled her impossibly closer, snaring her waist with one strong arm and stroking up her neck with his free hand, his fingers curling around her nape to cradle her head.

She'd have to be dead not to feel the unabashed sexual charge that sparked in the air. And, like a stick of dynamite, her insides detonated in an explosion of desire, sending an avalanche of wet heat thundering through her.

Quaking, she had to bite down hard on her lip to stifle a whimper. It didn't quite work. She let slip a hum-like cry.

Those dark, fathomless eyes locked onto her, pupils flaring as she swept her tongue across her bottom lip, and from nowhere a memory cracked through the brume of her mind...

Luciana was perched on a brick wall, waiting for him to lift her down, waiting for him to make his first move. Just...*waiting* for him. As if that was all she'd done all her life. 'Aren't you going to kiss me?' she'd asked, yearning for him to do just that.

When his expression had morphed into a giddy blend of enthusiasm and alarm she'd been flummoxed.

'Haven't you ever kissed a woman before?'

A blush so faint she'd nearly missed it had crept over the carved slash of his cheeks. A little embarrassed. A whole lot nervous.

She'd slid down the wall to puddle at his feet. 'Can I kiss you, then?' she'd asked, smoothing his frown away with her fingertips, tucking his hair behind his ears. 'Would that be okay?'

Ignoring the rhythmic tic in his jaw, she'd pushed up on her toes and pressed her lips to his. Warm. Soft. And as sensual and commanding as the man himself. Because as soon as she'd coaxed his mouth open with a flick of her tongue he'd taken over with an instinct as old as time and claimed her in a sweet, devouring...

Luciana blinked back to the here and now—to the snow whirling around them on the chorus of the breeze, the frozen wet droplets peppering her face. To Thane's dark eyes, deep and hungry and shot with shards of amber, the power of their sexual pull crippling in its intensity.

'My jet is the other way, angel,' he drawled, as if her defiance had not only been expected but he found her as cute as a button because of it.

The urge to kick him made her rapidly freezing feet twitch.

Angel... He'd never called her that before. He must have sharpened his sinful seduction skills over the past few years. It was crazy for her to wish he'd only ever been hers. Just as she'd only ever been his. Crazy. Men needed sex every day, didn't they? This man certainly had. Up close to him like this, it was easy to remember the long, sultry days and hot nights. Twisted sheets damp with sweat. Sticky skin and the musky scent of their passion lingering in the air as he was controlled by a dark atavistic need to mark her again and again. The slight soreness that only made them desperate for more. Insatiable. Never getting enough.

The base of her abdomen clenched; her core twisted with want.

Oh, this was bad. Really, *really* bad.

'Thane, let me go,' she demanded, cursing inwardly at the feathery panting that accompanied her words. 'I'm not joking. This is not funny. I'm not coming with you and you can't make me.'

His dark eyes glittered with challenge and her blood thrummed through her veins. She was scandalous—that was what she was.

'You and I both know I can and I will. So, are you going

to walk or will I have to carry you over my shoulder?' he asked, his rich velvet voice doing nothing to hide the steely threat of his words.

Problem was, her heavy breasts chose that exact moment to glory in being crushed against him, and when a fleck of snow landed on his nose she had the strangest impulse to lick it off.

'Thane...' Lord, was *that* her voice? That breathless, wanton plea?

'Luciana...' he drawled, in a tone that said *Please be reasonable about this.*

It inched her temper into the red zone.

'Don't fight this. Don't fight *me*. You don't want to go back there.'

'But I *do* want to go back, Thane.'

'No, angel. You don't.'

Argh!

'I'll scream and that man over there will come running. I guarantee it.'

His mouth tipped at the corner in a devilish smirk. 'Go ahead and I will smother that gorgeous mouth of yours.'

A gasp hit the back of her throat. 'You wouldn't dare.'

'Want to find out?' he growled.

Shameful excitement made her heart thump frenetically. 'No, I don't,' she said, though her voice sounded like a flagrant whimper to her. So she strove for forceful. 'Definitely not. Now, let go of me.'

He tutted and shook his head. 'Try again, Luciana. And if you say it like you mean it, I just might.'

Ooh, he'd asked for this.

Writhing in his hold, she pushed and shoved at his chest, drew in a lungful of air for the scream building in her throat...

And his mouth crashed over hers, taking his words from threat to carnal promise.

Oh, hell. Don't kiss him back. Don't you dare.

Within seconds he'd captured her in his invisible force field, energy swirling, flowing around them like a mini-cyclone, and her breath unwound on a blissful sigh.

He cradled her to him with one hand cupping her nape and the other splayed at the small of her back, hauling her up against his hard groin as he tilted his head and ravished her mouth as if he owned her body and soul.

Wicked was the flavour that flooded her mouth. So sinful and debauched he was. Bad to the bone. And when he stroked past her lips with a teasing flick and then a languorous lick of his tongue, that was it. She melted against him—all molten lava. Followed the sculpted line of his shoulders with her greedy hands up the column of his neck and slipped them beneath his ears, into his hair. Hair she fisted, making him growl long and low, the sound vibrating through her on a violent tremor.

The earth was moving, she was sure. Then she figured out why when he lifted her high and coaxed her legs around his waist. Luciana wrapped herself around him and hooked her ankles at the small of his back until there wasn't a sliver of air between them. He palmed the rounded swells of her bottom, squeezing her to him, and the erotic sensation of his thick hard erection nudging her lace panties made her sex throb and weep. He felt *shockingly* good and she whimpered, shivered.

Though that might also have been because she was wet, soaked to her skin. But he seemed to know what she needed, and when warmth suffused her and he sat down…*somewhere*…she straddled his muscular legs, cuddling closer to burrow into his heat.

Never leaving her mouth, he tore at her sodden coat, yanking it down her arms, and then his hot hands were back, sliding up her cool bare legs, pushing her dress up to ruck it around her thighs. And when those depraved fingers dug into the flesh of her bottom, pulling her panties indecently tight, the tug and rub of lace against her swollen folds made her cry out.

Survival instincts kicking in, she tore her lips free and dragged air into her lungs. Took a mind-numbing rush of his potent scent too. And that made her woozy. Impelled her to arch her back in a promiscuous plea for him to nuzzle her throat.

'Luciana…'

His lush, moist kisses fell on her skin like rain on drought-stricken ground and she soaked up every caress, thirsting for more. It had been so long since she'd been touched, since this man had touched her. So wonderful. Such naughty, amoral bliss.

'Thane…'

Dipping her head, she searched for his mouth and he dusted his lips over hers, teasing her cruelly. He tasted of pure virile masculinity, undiluted power. Passion and heat and lust and *Thane*.

Needing to touch, she ripped at the top buttons of his shirt, relishing his raspy curse and the sound of fabric tearing, and dived into the space she'd made, smoothing over his collarbone. Felt his heart beat a rapid staccato against her palm.

'Hot,' she whispered past his lips. 'So hot.'

His chest rumbled with a reply and yet she didn't hear a word, because a weird whooshing noise was blowing through her brain. Before she could grasp the why and the how, he scraped his stubble up the curve of her jaw in a sensual graze, making her tremble and rock her achingly heavy pelvis against him. Wanting his hardness inside her so, *so* badly.

When he let loose a feral moan from deep in his throat she did it again. And again. Her frenzied elation ratcheted up when his thumb slipped around her hip to find her sweet spot unerringly and apply just the right amount of pressure to take her to the edge of an almighty orgasm and hold her there.

'Thane, *please*.'

'*Dios*, Luciana… No bed in here, angel. But I want you to come for me. Hard. I want to hear you cry out my name like you used to.'

'Yes. *Yes…*'

Hold on.

Here? No bed *in here*?

He circled that tight knot of needy nerves and it took everything she had not to tumble into the abyss.

Her lashes were fluttering and her surroundings came to her in flashes. Cream leather seats. Small windows. Like a… like a private jet. And…were they moving?

Moving?

Luciana jerked backwards, dislodging his hand, blinking frantically, prising her eyes wide, her gaze darting here there and everywhere.

'What…? Where…? How…?'

She was the only one who was confused and disorientated, she noticed. Because the man whose lap she straddled simply sat there, his chest heaving from their passionate antics, cheeks streaked with colour, watching her with an insufferable blend of satisfaction and wariness.

Down she came, back to earth with shattering intensity. And how she didn't raise her hand and slap his face she'd never know.

'You…you *bastard*.'

Wrenching free, she tumbled backwards off his knee and landed in a messy, graceless heap. Still trembling from the erotic turbulence.

Thane lurched forward in a move to help.

'Don't you *dare* touch me.' Tears of frustration and anger pooled in her eyes.

Cautiously, he eased back into his chair, a deep V slashing the space between his brows. The look on her face must have said it all, she realised, since this was the first time he'd backed off at her word.

Somehow she clambered to her feet and stood tall before him, sweeping her palms down her black sheath, trying to cover as much of herself as she could before that horrid, vulnerable feeling of being exposed and raw threatened to strip her flesh from her bones.

Fury and self-disgust roiled inside her. Didn't diminish even when she saw a flicker of doubt and unease pass over his face. Though he soon banked it. It didn't matter. She would make him rue this day if it was the last thing she did.

'Luciana—'

'No. *Don't* speak to me.'

Spine pin-straight, she walked towards the other large leather recliner, trying to wrap her mind around her new predicament. What on earth was she going to do now? She—

A thought slammed into her, and she whirled back on a swirling spin of dizzying dread. 'My bag,' she said, unable to hide the panic in her voice. 'Where's my handbag?'

He was staring out of the small window, rubbing his mouth with the inside of his finger. 'Sit down, Luciana, we are about to take off.'

'No, dammit, I *won't*!'

Shucking off his wet jacket, he kept his eyes averted. 'Did you leave it in the car?'

Oh; God.

Her stomach pitched as the jet lifted off the runway, and she grabbed the back of the chair to keep from crumpling to the carpet.

'Go back down. Land this plane. Right now, Thane. I need my bag. My phone. I *need* my phone.'

How was she going to call Natanael? Keep in touch with home? Text Nate as she did every morning, noon and night?

Desperation made her beg the man she loathed with every ounce of her being. 'Thane, *please*, I need my phone.'

He didn't turn, still wouldn't look at her. Just inhaled deeply and closed his eyes for a beat. 'Where we are going no phone of yours will even work, Luciana. Sit down and leave it.'

She gritted her teeth, mightily glad for the return of that cool, dominant inflection because it evaporated the acidic splash behind her eyes. She would not break. Not in front of this man. Nor any other.

'I hate you right now,' she whispered vehemently. Though she suspected she hated herself even more.

One kiss. That was all it had taken to vanquish every thought from her mind.

Self-loathing slithered through her stomach to writhe like a nest of vipers and she curled into the deep bucket seat to ease the ache.

No phone. No way to call Nate. No chance of escape. And she was flying straight into enemy territory.

If she got through this in one piece and found her way home it would be a miracle.

CHAPTER FIVE

HE FELT LIKE the big bad wolf. In more ways than one. Furious self-censure and unparalleled carnal hunger took equal pleasure in tearing at his insides with razor-sharp claws until he wanted to growl.

The lust made his body thrum with pent-up energy, yet all he wanted to do was storm over there, pick her up and put her right back on his knee. Eradicate the pain in her eyes by wrapping her up in his arms and holding her tightly to him.

Dios, when tears had glistened in those big, beautiful eyes he'd felt as if a bullet had ripped clean through his chest. He'd been a little boy again, looking up at his mother, unsure what to do, how to take her heartache away. A heartache that once again he didn't truly understand. And that had made him feel lost. Racking his brains to think of some way to stem her misery. Because somehow his mother had always managed to quell his, take his pain away—back when his flesh could feel such a sensation, that was.

Rubbing over his jaw, he recalled how touching her had often worked—holding her cold, trembling hand or trying to wrap his small, thin arms around her shoulders to hug her, wishing he was bigger, stronger. Instinctively he'd reached for Luciana, but she didn't want his touch. While he'd always treasured hers. Touch was precious to him, he realised. Infinitely rare and beyond price, it was something he hadn't experienced or allowed himself to feel since he'd been seven years old. Until Luciana.

'I hate you...'

How her words tormented him. How her tears made him feel barbaric. As brutal as his father.

While he still owned what he'd had to do, he conceded his tactics might not have been the most honourable. Had he been wrong to take his chance? Hell, no. Not when the alternative was her marrying another man. A man she didn't even wish to marry! Still, luring her onto a flight using their chemistry, when she'd exploded like some hot, sensual, sultry bomb in his hands, and then almost initiating them into the ranks of the mile-high club wasn't exactly coaxing her towards a priest with a gentle hand, was it?

The memory of her furiously wild, uninhibited passion made him shift in his seat with restless virile power—as if his body had lain dormant for an age of cold bleak winters and she'd awoken the deep-seated animalistic lust inside him.

And right then the truth crashed down around him.

For the first time in years he was feeling, and he was chasing it with the urgency and fervour of a madman. He felt hungry, starved of affection, and suddenly he despised it. Didn't want her to have that kind of terrific power over him. He'd had more control when he'd been handed his first gun at twelve.

Lurching from his seat, he went to stalk to his office, where he could think straight, past the chair where she sat curled up, knees bent, hugging them to her chest, in a pose that struck him as a defensive ball—and he slammed to a stop.

Thumb-print-shaped blotches reddened her silky soft thighs, courtesy of his rough ardour, and her neck was scored pink from where he'd kissed her, dragged his unshaven jaw up her delicate throat. Ravaged. She looked ravaged.

Dios, had he hurt her?

He closed his eyes, his conscience riven by self-contempt. Maybe he didn't deserve to have her in his life again.

He could never be good inside, where it mattered. That had been twisted out of him as a boy. He was darkness and she was all golden light.

Good versus evil. Beautiful versus beastly. Flawless versus scarred.

Fatigue lent a beautiful fragility to her face. And when a shiver rustled over her honey-gold skin his guts twisted tight. She looked scared, miserable and *attacked*. So damn vulnerable.

Idiot he was—of course she'd be worried. While they'd spent one month in each other's arms there were years of animosity between their countries.

Opening one of the top cupboards, he pulled down some thick fluffy blankets and lowered into a crouch before her.

Her little bow-shaped mouth was mutinous in her heart shaped face. 'Get away from me, Thane.'

'Luciana,' he said, his voice rich and smooth, 'I am sorry I've upset you this badly.'

'*Upset* me?'

She flared up with spectacular force—his ferocious little lioness. He actually felt himself blanch when he saw her eyes, pools of brandy swimming in betrayal.

'Oh, just go away. I'm not speaking to you.'

'You just did,' he said lazily, trying to lighten the mood, get her to come round to him.

'Only because you're forcing me to. You are such a control freak. Do you get off on being Mr Big and Powerful? Taking away people's choices?'

That wasn't what he'd done. Was it…?

'No, what I was doing was preventing you from making a mistake. Giving you freedom from your father. You owe him nothing, angel. Soon you'll realise I've done you a great favour, and when you thank me I will not be so arrogant as to say *I told you so*.'

Moaning, as if his very existence was painful to her, she

squeezed her eyes shut and banged her head on the headrest. 'You're impossible. You really are.'

Gingerly, he covered her in layers of dove-grey cashmere and tucked the ends underneath her.

'What's this? A peace offering?' she jeered.

'No, a blanket,' he drawled as he slipped off her towering white glossy shoes. Unable to resist that ticklish spot, he ran his thumb over the sexy little nub of her anklebone.

She flinched and tucked her foot under the blanket, rebuffing him.

Thane sighed, stood tall, and shunted a hand through his hair. Back to that place where he was lost. Only knowing in that moment that making her smile at him was more important than anything else. And that thought was not only unnerving but also perilous and highly confusing.

His office silently chanted his name.

'I'll leave you for a while, then,' he said, stepping away.

Naturally that was when she started ranting all over him.

'How do you *do* this to me, Thane? How do you make me want you and hate you at the same time? I have no sense when it comes to you. None!'

One fat tear slipped down her cheek and his cold, stony heart cracked in two.

'Now look at the mess I'm in.'

The desolate anguish in her voice made him remember, and he couldn't just stand there paralysed. He had to do that in his own country, almost every damn day.

Ah, to hell with it.

Swooping in, he scooped her up...

'Hey!'

He turned and plonked them both back down in her seat, holding her close.

'I...I told you not to touch me again,' she choked out, trying to fight him and her tears at the same time. 'Honest to God, do you listen to one single, solitary thing I say?'

Palm to her cheek, he pushed at the side of her face to

nestle her into his neck. 'It may not seem so, but, yes. I just… Let me hold you. Warm you up. Please? Just for a moment. You're shivering.'

He tucked the blanket tightly around her, from her sexy knees to the feminine slope of her nose, until she was swaddled, unable to move an inch.

'There you go. You look like a cute furry Egyptian mummy, but that's better, *si*?'

If looks could kill, he'd be dead.

'It may be better if you remove that damp dress from your skin,' he suggested.

It was shrinking by the second, he was sure. He was also sure he wanted it off her, since he could easily conjure up far more pleasurable ways to make his thoughtless arrogance up to her.

Hiking her chin up over the cashmere, she harrumphed at him. '*As. If.* Now you're trying to get my clothes off? Forget it, Romeo. This Juliet isn't falling for that.'

Thane frowned. 'They were enemies, weren't they?'

'Yeah… Ring any bells? And there was no happy ending for them either. She killed herself, so let that be a lesson to you.'

Spine rigid, he stiffened up…then slammed down the memory before it invaded him and the blackness tainted his soul. No, that would *never* happen with Luciana. She was not his mother. He and Luciana had history. He'd made her happy once and he would again. He was a man now—stronger, more powerful—he would be enough this time. Wouldn't he?

'Thane?' she squeaked. 'Can you let me breathe? You're squashing me, here. Are you trying to suffocate me now? First you abduct me and now you're squeezing me to death. Frankly, I'm not too sure if you even *like* me, so why you'd want to marry me is beyond my comprehension.'

'Ah, sorry, angel.'

He loosened his hold a touch and nuzzled a kiss into her

hair while he could—while she was wrapped up and couldn't protest or reject him.

'Of course I like you,' he said. 'I'll have you know I don't go around kissing just anyone.' Speaking of kissing… 'Did I hurt you earlier? Was I too rough?'

The luxurious spill of her hair tumbled over one shoulder, a shimmering flow of dark bronze that Thane swept back from her face tenderly.

Those absurdly long lashes fluttered, yet she prised her eyes wide, fighting it. Fighting *him*. It just made him want her all the more.

'Yes, you hurt me. Inside you hurt me. And I'll never forgive you for that stunt you just pulled.'

'Admittedly I didn't think it would backfire in such a spectacular fashion,' he drawled, trying his utmost to ease the tension he could feel coiling in her body. Her luscious, curvy weight was glorious, he decided. 'Would you consider that I thought your tongue down my throat meant yes?'

'No, I most certainly would not.'

The haughty lash of her riposte made him retaliate with his equally devilish mouth. 'What about the way you rode my lap?'

Her lips parted on a stunned smack. 'Lord, you really *are* wicked.' Punching at the blanket for some wriggle room, she shoved at his chest. 'Go away. Go and take your guilt elsewhere. I'm not pacifying it for you. You deserve it.'

'Who says I feel guilty?'

He did. Terribly. He might have wanted to lure and beguile her, but upset her this much? No. That was the last thing he'd wanted. It made him wonder if he was missing something vital. Surely being rescued from a repulsive royal marriage was something to celebrate, not to weep over.

'I can see it all over your face. And you *should* feel guilty too. I told you I was not getting on this plane, but did you listen? Of course you didn't. Then I begged you to go back for my bag, my phone…' Sighing heavily, she thumped her head back down on his shoulder. 'I hate you.'

'So you said. But, like *I* said, your cell phone would not have worked in Galancia. At least nowhere near the castle.'

Like Fort Knox with scrambling systems, its obscene opulence was locked up tight.

And right then, for the first time, he thought of his birthright and doubt slithered its sinuous way up his spine. Not only did he loathe the place but also his uncle… He didn't want his uncle anywhere near Luciana. Because as soon as his uncle set eyes on her he'd know Thane planned to overthrow him and doubtless stir up trouble.

To hell with that. He needed Luciana to say *I do* first. And to get her there he needed time. Time only for them. When he wasn't distracted by having to peer over his shoulder.

Glaring up at him with a fierceness that verged on the adorable, she mocked, 'My phone wouldn't work in the castle? Truth or lie?'

A laugh burst past his lips—one he hadn't heard in an age. For a woman who had been in Zurich to let loose and have *fun*, she remembered quite a bit. 'Truth. Swear it. Why do you want your phone so badly?'

She flung her now unencumbered arm out in front of them, exasperated, missing his face by an inch.

'Why do you think? My family will be beside themselves with worry by morning and it's heartless of you not to care.'

He *was* heartless. Completely heartless. Yet every time he thought of that single tear he didn't want to be. Not for her. And that was akin to tying a garrotte around his own neck. By opening up he would give her the power to destroy him again, and he couldn't go through that a second time. It would kill him. No, he had to keep his head straight and focus on his end goal. The crown.

But, unlike him, Luciana had a huge heart, and he didn't want her fretting about her family so he'd have to fix that too. He didn't want her mind on anything else but him.

'Are we talking about the same family who is pushing you into an arranged marriage that you don't want?' he asked.

'First off, what *you* have offered isn't much different.'

She had a point there. What could he give her in a marriage that Augustus couldn't? Just as he despised Henri for dragging her towards matrimony, he didn't intend to do that either.

Which begged the question—how was he going to entice her there?

'Maybe it isn't. But that man will never be in your bed as long as I live and breathe.'

'Neanderthal, much?'

He gave a breezy shrug. She could call him what she liked; it changed nothing.

'And, secondly, I'm not merely talking about my father. I'm talking about my sister, Claudia. She'll be frantic by morning.' A devious light flashed in her eyes. 'Speaking of Claudia... Oh, you don't want to meet *her* husband in a dark alley. In fact when he hears about this he'll make you wish you'd never been born.'

Thane lounged back with a lazy smile on his face. 'This would be Lucas Garcia? Once head of national security for Arunthia?'

'That's exactly who it is.'

'And you think *I* fear *him*?'

She scrunched up her nose. 'Yes, well, come to think of it that *is* a flawed strategy. The devil himself wouldn't scare *you*. But one day you're going to meet your nemesis, and I'd love to be there when you do.'

He had a feeling he already had. In this woman.

'If I have my way you *will* be there.'

'On this occasion I'm afraid you'll have to accept defeat. I'm not staying with you. I'll move heaven and earth to get home, and the sooner you realise that the better. You can't always have what you want, Thane.'

'Ah, Luciana. When there is a war to be fought I will always be the victor. Especially when I want the prize so very, very badly. And I want *you*, Luciana—very, *very* badly. So I will do whatever it takes to make you mine.'

Those smooth, satiny cheeks flooded with a warm sensual blush of pleasure even as she pursed her mouth in an expression that screamed cynicism.

'Whatever it takes, huh? I don't think personality transplants are available on this continent, Thane. And, believe me, it will take more than a dishonourable kidnapping rat to woo me down the aisle.'

At the blatant challenge he felt his blood heat and he arched one brow.

'Okay. So I haven't been the most noble of men today.'

'Ha!'

'I honestly didn't think it would upset you this much. I am struggling to understand why you want to go home so desperately when there is nothing for you there but a ball and chain and a vapid viscount.'

She shifted uneasily and pulled her lip into her moist mouth with a scrape of her teeth. Before he could discern if he was seeing guilt or not, she ground that curvy, firm bottom over his rapidly hardening groin and he had to grind his jaw to stop a feral moan escaping.

Unclamping his jaw took some effort. 'All that being said, perhaps a more subtle approach *would* have been better— but I cannot turn back time.'

'You could take me home,' she suggested hopefully.

Not if the survival of mankind depended on it.

'What about if I make a deal with you instead?'

That grabbed her attention, and she focused those incredible eyes back on him. Where he wanted them to stay.

'What kind of a deal?'

'You give me two days to…what did you call it? Court you? Date you? And if after those two days you still wish to return home I will take you myself. Escort you to your father's door and never darken it again.'

Not that it would come to that.

The knowledge that he was using military tactics to keep his princess in line did not impress his sense of fair play, but then again fair play had flown out of the window when he'd clapped eyes on her in the company of Augustus. She was his gorgeous little lioness. The answer to his royal prayers.

In his arms, he could feel the tension ooze from her body, and a corresponding flood of gratification unravelled the anxious knots in his mind.

'You mean it?'

Her brandy eyes melted to warm honey and flowed through his chest like blissful nectar, soothing his every raw nerve. He brushed the back of his index finger down her nose. Over her lips. Luscious lips that he glossed with the pad of his thumb, where they were still bruised from his kisses.

A new kind of tension sizzled in the air and a glow of unsatisfied desire filled the space between them—an invisible presence that moved over his skin, sliding over them both like a caress. A teasing, taunting, tempting caress.

And right *there* was the difference between him and Augustus. Bedevilled, off-the-charts sizzling chemistry. Black magic.

This. This was what he would play on.

Regardless of how he'd got her on this jet, he still made her weak with desire—and right now that was all he had to work with.

Rebelling against the inner voice warning him to stop, to keep his head this time and cajole her with a gentle hand, he brought his mouth to the edge of her ear and closed his teeth around her lobe.

Her breathless panting whispered over his neck and made his pulse thrash against his cuff. It was a low, husky carnal want that made him murmur, 'Absolutely I mean it. I swear it on my very life.'

Two days were all he needed to lure her over to the dark side.

'Let me show you the most beautiful place on earth.'

He knew the perfect spot for the ultimate seduction, where his Queen would surrender right into his waiting arms.

'What do say, angel?'

CHAPTER SIX

LUCIANA WAS IN the throes of a wonderful dream and she never wanted to wake up. Amazingly strong, muscular arms wrapped her in the warmth of their protection and the rhythmic sound of the ocean lapping over the shore lulled her mind into a tranquil peace she hadn't felt in aeons.

A muffled lyrical trill shattered the halcyon bliss and beckoned her to rouse.

Bright was the splash of daylight behind her eyelids. Soft and sensually luxurious was the satin beneath her tummy and her cheek. Sweet was the scent of buttery pastry…or possibly French toast.

The musical chime hushed to a harmonious end.

Luciana writhed on the deeply cushioned mattress and stretched the kinks from her body, then prised her eyes open once, twice—and bolted up on all fours.

'Where the—?'

Rocking back, she sat on her ankles, her heart thrashing a symphonic staccato as her gaze bounced around the gargantuan almond-white room.

Holy-moly…

Paradise. She was in an enormous satin-drenched bed in paradise. Not only that, it felt inordinately pure. Minimalistic, all in varying shades of white, it serenaded a desperate search for solace.

In front of her and behind were the only solid walls, and when she swung to her right Luciana gasped at the fifty-foot-wide unencumbered view of a beautiful azure sky and the glistening crystalline waters of the Med as it frolicked with champagne sands. It was as if the entire wall had been rolled back and hidden to one side.

A wide wooden deck ran from the room to the shoreline and she smiled when a small lizard scurried across the sun-drenched teak.

Flipping her gaze to the left, to the opposite open expanse, she was faced with a rugged slab of rock dyed a deep charcoal-grey by the waterfall that sluiced down from some great height she couldn't see, to rush and froth and pool, then run beneath this very room…out through the other side and down toward the beach. Under the deck, she'd guess.

Gripping the edge of the bed, she tipped over to look at the floor, her hair spilling around her face. *Oh, wow.* Glass. The entire floor was glass. And she watched a vivid kaleidoscope of teeny-tiny fish dip and swerve and play beneath her.

So beautiful.

Giddiness leapt inside her at the sheer awesome natural beauty of it all—stunning architecture and a visual feast for the senses had always fascinated her. Odd that Thane was probably the only man she'd ever told that too.

Speaking of Thane… She lurched back upright to sit on the bed. Where the heck was he? And her heart-rate did *not* shoot through the roof when she thought of his name. Absolutely not. She hated the man. Yes, she did.

That would be the Thane who'd appeared so desperate to carry her into the main house, since by the time they'd arrived her insides had been battered and bruised from pummelling emotions and she'd been shivering with exhaustion. The Thane who had lain her gently in his bed…and after that everything was a bit blurry. Oh, Lord. Was it too much to ask that she'd booted him out of the room and banished him to Hades? Of course it was.

But, in her defence, her barricades had been low. And the devil was a maestro at taking advantage of that.

Lingering anger had her fisting the sheets.

She might have agreed to this bargain—*ha!* Agreed? As if she'd had *any* choice. But he was in for a nasty shock—because she was only here to prove she'd be the wife from hell. She'd evict him from her mind for ever while she focused on her end-game. Getting home to Natanael, come hell or high water.

On the plus side, seeing the real dark Prince in action, embroiled in some villainous scheme, would be just the ticket to satisfy her conscience that she'd made the right choices for them all. To ameliorate the guilt that constantly ate at her insides because she was keeping her son's existence a secret.

Though, honestly, she was mad even to trust that he'd take her home in two days. But the alternative was hauling out the big guns—her father. Who would likely kick off a military invasion. And that was the last thing she wanted. Hence she'd surrendered to the dark Prince.

Certifiable? Probably.

The opening bars of muffled Mozart trilled through the room—*again!*—and Luciana vaulted off the bed, the bare pads of her feet hitting cool glass as she searched every table-top. Because that sounded suspiciously like her phone. Which made no sense considering he'd told her it wouldn't work anywhere near the castle. But maybe he'd changed his mind about taking her there, maybe they were miles away from the horrid place—

'Oh, good Lord. My bag!' She'd never been so darn happy in her life! She could *kiss* that horrible brute right now.

Snatching the black leather heap from the side table, she shoved her hand in, rummaging to the bottom.

'Don't ring off…don't stop. *Please* don't stop ringing.'

Shaking like a windswept leaf, she barely managed to hit 'accept' and mash it to her ear.

'H…Hello?'

'*Luciana?*' Claudia's voice was a sound for sore ears. 'Thank God—where are you?'

'I'm…'

Common sense smacked her upside the head. Where the blazes was Thane? She didn't want him party to this conversation.

'Hold on a minute,' she whispered frantically as she ducked and dived all over the room, opening and closing doors, her heart slamming around her chest, feeling like an extra out of a badly acted eighties cop show.

Aha! There he was. The fiend. In the distance, standing on the beach, talking to a short dark-haired man. Throwing a stick into the water, of all things.

Unleashing a pent-up breath, she slumped where she stood. Looked pretty innocent to her. No dastardly guns drawn or fisticuffs. *Yet.*

'Okay, I can talk. Is Nate all right?' she whispered, stepping back out of sight, hoping the walls didn't have ears. Or maybe she was on camera. Her gaze darted around the four upper corners of the room just in case.

'Of course he's all right. He's out with Lucas and Isabelle. Now, for heaven's sake, where *are* you?'

Good question. She actually couldn't believe she was about to say this. 'I'm in…Galancia.'

'*Galancia?*'

Claudia's holler had Luciana wrenching the phone from her almost burst eardrum.

'Oh. my God. I thought Augustus had been smoking pot or something.'

'The only thing Augustus gets high on is women.'

'*Eww.* He didn't? When you were *there*?'

'Sure he did.'

'You can't marry that man, Luce.'

Oh, great—Claudia sounded like Thane. Thane who wanted her '*very, very badly*'.

Luciana rubbed the heel of her hand over her left breast.

Naïve fool that she was, she wanted to believe those three little words. Words that whispered to a secret place inside her. So it was fortunate that his mind-blowing pheromones hadn't obliterated her every brain cell. Obviously he wanted something from her—everyone always did. She just wasn't sure what.

'Did Augustus tell Father?' she asked.

'No, not yet. Lucas made him keep his mouth shut until we heard from you. Half of me wondered if you'd just ducked out on Augustus, so we were giving you today to contact us before raising the alarm. Especially with Dad the way he is. Luce, what were you *thinking*, going there with that man?'

'I didn't have much choice.'

She stormed around the room, shaking the kinky mess from her ratty locks. *Ugh*, she felt gross. And *that* was when she spied her case on a pale ecru velvet chaise longue. *Her case!*

Mid jiggy-dance, she froze as every ounce of blood drained to her toes. Had he searched it? Hauling it from the chaise, she plonked it on the end of the bed and fumbled with the lock. The still locked lock. *Phew.*

Shoulders slumping, she tuned back in to Claudia's voice.

'What do you mean, you didn't have much choice? Did he force you? Did he…*kidnap* you? *Did he*?'

Claudia's glorious indignation flew down the phone line, and it was so good having someone in her corner. She took a great gulp of air to rake him over the hot coals…

And her gaze crashed into the wide stretch of canvas over the carved bedstead, making the words jam in her throat.

'Oh.'

'What do you mean "oh"? Luce, did you hear me?'

'Yes—yes, I heard you. Sorry, Claudia.'

'Did that Galancian brute *steal* you? *Did* he? That's it. I'm sending Lucas over there right now. He'll raze that place to the ground and get you out—'

'No.' What was she doing? *What are you doing, Luce...?*
'No, he didn't take me, Claudia. I...I agreed to come.'

'Mmm-hmm. You sure about that?'

'Yes. He...he asked me to stay with him a couple of days to...talk. Yes, to talk. Then he's bringing me home.'

'Mmm-hmm.'

'Honest.'

Claudia's voice softened. 'Luciana, darling, do you really know what you're doing?'

Lifting her hand, she pressed her fingers over her mouth, felt them tremble against her lips, unable to take her eyes off the picture in front of her.

'Not really. But now I'm here I need to know. I need to...' *Prove to myself I'm over him. Make sure I've done the right thing.*

'Okay, I hear you. Even the stuff you're not saying. The feelings that put that desolate look in your eyes...they haven't gone, huh?'

'No,' she whispered. *They scare me.* 'And that's ruinous, Claudia, because he's bad for me. He's dangerous. I'm reckless with him. He makes me want to be wicked. I spiral out of control. And I can't do that because I have to protect—'

'Luce. You know who you sound like, right? If there is one thing our father is good at it's the old brainwashing technique. Stop listening to his voice. It isn't wicked to want. Maybe...' She let loose a heavy sigh. 'Maybe these two days are exactly what you need. But that's all I can give you before I have to tell Father. Though with his weak heart I'd rather send Lucas in.'

'It'll be like the clash of the titans.'

'My money is on Lucas,' Claudia said, in the confident, proud way only a wife madly in love could.

And there was Luciana with her money on Thane. What that said about her she wouldn't like to guess.

'Just...call me whenever you can, okay?'

'Okay.' Luciana sneaked another peek outside, to check

he still loitered on the beach. 'What has Nate been doing?' she whispered achingly. She missed him so much.

'Playing with Isabelle, painting, making his list for Santa. You name it. He's as happy as a pig in muck. Don't worry. You weren't due back for a couple more days anyway. He's just munching his way through his advent calendar and waiting for his present from your trip since that's before the big day.'

Luciana smiled, glancing down at her case. The case Thane must have sent for. How *dared* he send her into another freefall when she'd just started detesting him?

'I have it for him. Will you tell him I'll text later and that I love him, Claudia? Please?'

'Of course I will. He knows you do. That little boy is rolling in love.'

But not the love of a daddy. Had she ever allowed herself to acknowledge that? No. Because she'd always thought that was something she couldn't give him.

Throat raw and swollen, her words hurt. 'I'll keep in touch, Claudia, I promise.'

'Be careful, Luce.'

At the dead tone Luciana tossed her phone to the bed and tilted her head, her hair sliding over her shoulder as she stared at the past.

Predator-like, stealthy footsteps sounded across the deck and her nefarious blood thrummed in exhilaration. Then his alluring scent hit her, courtesy of the ocean breeze: dark and divine and oh-so-drugging.

'*Buenos dias.*' Rich with heat and layered in sin, that voice curled around her body in a hot, hungry embrace, making her shiver with want.

Somehow he'd sucked all the oxygen from the vast expanse, so when she took a deep breath to peek at him and came up short the room did a crazy little spin. 'G...Good morning.'

A glorious full-bodied smile kicked his lips up and her

heart into gear. And—*oh, Lord*—that solitary dimple she adored so much…The iridescent lustre of happiness in his black sapphire eyes… As if seeing her here, in his home, was the best sight in the world.

All it took was one long look and the burning butterfly in her stomach fluttered its wings, enflaming her mind with reckless, shameless abandon. Didn't they always say the real enemy was within? Ah, yes… Her body—the traitor.

He carded his fingers through his tousled raven-black hair and she was inclined to think he'd spent the morning at a magazine photo shoot for sex incarnate.

Suave black suit trousers hugged his mighty fine muscular legs, and he'd paired them with a slim-fit crisp white open-collared shirt for a look that oozed sinful gravitas and delectable danger. But that wasn't the worst of it. *Nooo*, of course it wasn't. Because the universe had it in for her, remember? So of course the delicious brute was clean-shaven, and that sexy scarred divot in his chin begged to be licked and kissed as she stroked that smooth jaw.

Groaning inwardly, she crossed her arms and winced when she chafed her heavy, sensitive breasts. *Darn it*. The man knew it too. Cocking one dark brow as if he knew precisely what he did to her. The wretch.

'It was wonderful to wake up with you in my arms again, Luciana.'

Her stomach did a slow, languorous roll. 'Oh, really? Did you do that without permission too?'

Mock affront widened his deep, devastating eyes. 'Absolutely not. In fact I had every intention of sleeping elsewhere. But you refused to let me go.'

'I…I did?'

He nodded with deep satisfaction and tutted, as if she'd been very, *very* naughty. 'You were most displeased when I tried to move this morning.'

Heat exploded in her cheeks. 'Obviously I thought I was

in bed with someone else.' Surely that would set off his cave-man alarm bells and twitch his temper?

Except all he did was take a lethal step towards her. And another. Until she felt hunted, pursued, desired beyond measure.

'No, it was definitely *my* name you were calling in that sexy purr of yours.'

He spoke with a debauched rasp and frisked his prurient gaze down the length of her, snagging it on her chest. His gaze was covetous. Heated.

And *that* was when she realised she was wearing only her black lacy camisole and panties.

'Oh, Lord…'

She yanked a loose, rumpled almond sheet from the bed—the bed *they* had slept in—and hastily wrapped it around her, toga style.

'There is nothing I haven't seen before, Luciana,' he growled, his voice thick with lust as he stepped up close.

'Th…That's not the point.'

Up came his arm and he tucked a lock of hair behind her ear—his touch as light and feathery as dandelion fluff—then trailed one licentious fingertip down her throat…over her décolletage…whispering scandalous promises to her flesh.

'Nothing I haven't stroked or licked or sucked or kissed before either. And I cannot wait to do all of those things again.'

Her core twisted with want even as panic shot down her spine. Was he trying to seduce her? Oh, no. No way. He wasn't doing this to her again. She would *not* surrender a second time. Regardless of that dissolute brooding certainty.

'I'm not giving you the chance.'

'Is that right?' he drawled with a devilish smile, as if the mere suggestion that she could resist him was delightfully droll. *Horrid man*.

Luciana stumbled back a step and hauled the white shift

dress she'd taken to Courchevel to wear by the pool out of her case.

All fumbling arms, she wrestled herself into the dress and wriggled from the sheet, rambling to cover her discomfort. 'And, actually, there's plenty you haven't seen before. Twelve whole pounds of plenty. And despite what my mother says about curves being out of fashion, and how I'm not setting a very good example, I'm owning every one of them. Because one: I can't get shot of them, no matter how much I starve, and being hungry really is no picnic. And two: every single one of those pounds was worth the—'

'Worth the...?'

Closing her eyes for a beat, she realised everything was too raw, too close to the surface. She felt like a tiny volcano that could erupt at the wrong word or look and spew forth the burning destructive truth.

'Those...' She twizzled her index finger, making a little circle in the air. 'Round American chocolatey crunchy biscuits with cream in the middle. Can't remember what they're called off the top of my head.'

'Then when I meet *these*...' he twirled his finger too '...round American chocolatey crunchy biscuits with cream in the middle, I shall thank them personally. They look good on you.'

'They do?'

Aw, Luce, what did you ask him that for?

'Better than good.' He licked his lips, as if tasting her would be just as sweet and luscious. 'Fabulous.'

Yeah, right.

'Wow, considering how we ended up in bed the first time...' In short, she'd had to beguile him into undressing her—not exactly ladylike behaviour. 'Your repertoire for seduction skills really *has* come on.'

His smile was full of virile disrepute. 'You only have yourself to blame. I was inaugurated and taught by the best, after all.'

Imagine who'd been slain in his bed ever since he speared her with a warped arrow of pain and pique. 'Then clearly I created a monster.'

Laughter rumbled up from the depths of his chest. 'I think you did, angel.'

With that, he glanced up at the canvas stretched across the wall and his smile faltered.

'Right there. It's a good likeness—a stunning rendition. Don't you think?'

She had to swallow around the great lump in her throat. 'Yes, it is. It's…beautiful, Thane.'

Why? Why did he have a painting of their favourite spot in Zurich? Where they'd stayed. A dramatic panorama of the Rhine Falls. Luciana could virtually hear the roaring rush of water, feel the moist mist peppering her skin, see the craggy jutting rocks, the Prussian blue lakes.

'Do you remember the day we met?' he asked distractedly. He stared at the scene with a deep frown. As if it was the first time he'd allowed himself to really look at it.

To remember was to open a vault she'd bolted shut years ago. A perilous endeavour, just as dangerous as he was. But, as always, this man silenced the screams of her self-preservation.

'If you hadn't walked by that day…' Scary to think what might have happened.

'What were you doing there, Luciana?'

'Celebrating the end of finals.'

She'd caved in to temptation and jetted across Europe with some trusted friends from her politics class. And while her father had been under the illusion that she'd remain in London for another month, Luciana had gone incognito and ventured into her first foray into rebellion.

She'd been intoxicated by the heady taste of absolute freedom. One she'd failed to find at university, as she'd hoped. Eyes had still watched and reported back to her parents. Gossip had still fuelled the press. But in Zurich, for the first time in her life, she'd been a normal person. A woman the paparazzi wouldn't look at twice. Lost in the crowd and having the time of her life.

Until a two-hundred-pound strung-out Viking had cornered her behind a tour bus, the foul scent of beer leaching from his every pore, wanting some 'fun' of his own. And in those terrifying moments she'd cursed her naïve recklessness and prayed for someone to appear. For *this* man to appear.

It had been Thane who'd torn him off her and knocked him clean out with one punch. Thane, who'd locked onto her eyes and never let her go. Thane, who'd kept a careful distance as he'd walked her back to her apartment as if she were some fragile fawn.

The romantic little girl in her had called it serendipity. Thinking about it, dark and dangerous should have screamed at her to run, yet she'd been petrified that he'd leave. Take that awesome powerful protection with him. So she'd finagled him into having a coffee, then dinner, and drinks after that. And suddenly she'd been dependent, hooked on him like a drug, and all she'd craved was the next fix.

She'd been addicted to the intense highs. Though she'd do well to remember the aftermath. Horrendous heart-wrenching lows. Lost. Unfocused. She'd sworn she would never be dependent on another man.

Still… 'You saved me.'

'He is lucky to still walk the earth,' he said scathingly, in a fierce, low, dominant tone.

And she couldn't help it. She smiled wide—big and genuine and just for him. Because she'd been terrified and he'd been…*awesome*.

Eyes locked with his once more, she couldn't break free of his hold. They were drawn together like powerful magnets. As it had been from the start.

His initial confusion at their combustible attraction was unforgettable. As if he'd never known such passion and lust could exist. Endearing. Dazzling. He'd enslaved her in seconds.

Do you remember our first time? her heart whispered. *Yours? Mine? Teaching one another how to give pleasure and take? I remember every tender, evocative touch, every blissful second in your arms. The longing. The delirium as you drove deeper and deeper into my body until I felt indelibly marked. Branded. Claimed. Wanted. Desired.*

Yours.

Her heart ached, and Thane stared into her eyes as if the secrets of her soul were nothing more than words on a page.

Oh, Lord. She was in so much trouble here.

She was supposed to be reassuring herself that her secrets were better kept buried. Ensuring that Thane rued the day they'd ever met. Yet here she was, reminiscing about 'the good ol' times' and trying not to think of the damage they could do to the bed. They had busted a frame or two in their time…

What she *wasn't* supposed to be was more confused than ever. But within the space of ten minutes all her carefully erected defences were crumbling down around her, leaving her brain reduced to chaos and rubble.

And she hated it. Hated that the semblance of control she'd been hanging on to was as precarious as her future.

Luciana had to remember who he was and how exactly she came to be standing in his bedroom. Instead of musing that underneath, where it counted the most, he might still be the man she'd fallen for. And if that was true they were all in a bigger mess than she'd ever imagined. A wealth of pain at her hands. Because she was a mother and if her son could have a father who was a good man, hell would freeze before she kept them apart any longer.

Insides shaking, she tore her gaze from his. And as soon as that powerful connection was severed the fog began to clear.

Remember who he is, how you got here. How he once

tried to assassinate your father. Don't forget that you're enemies.

She had to stop listening to the longing of her heart. Get through the next two days unscathed, then run as fast as she could. Before she started doubting her own mind and cracked under the pressure. Told him the one secret that would change their lives for ever. The one secret she would never be able to take back.

CHAPTER SEVEN

DESPITE THE CLOAK of aloofness that suddenly settled over her, Thane had an incredibly light, airy feeling. Much like the five-foot dazzling iridescent aqua dolphin balloon he'd once bought Luciana. She'd adored the garish spectacle and, seeing that same gorgeous smile on her face moments ago— the one that made his heart kind of...*stop*—he'd known he'd played the perfect pitch by bringing her here.

She'd visibly relaxed since speaking to her sister—he'd heard her softly spoken goodbye and made a mental score to thank Seve for unearthing her case and bag pronto. By dusk today she would fall into his arms like a sweet ripe apple tumbling from a tree.

Already she was unravelling more by the second—nothing like the Princess who'd slid so gracefully into his car only yesterday. Rumpled. Tousled. Looking sublimely natural and sexed-up. No show or lipstick or pristine dress, she was sexier than anything he'd ever seen or, he suspected, would ever see in his lifetime.

He growled inwardly. Wanting her under him. Beneath him. Surrendering to him. Insane, she made him insane with want. But, as much as he knew she desired him with equal wanton abandon, something held her back, so he refused to rush this or lose his head.

Velvety rich, the scent of coffee and pastries wafted on the sultry breeze, and when Luciana's stomach grumbled

Thane satisfied himself that he could at least pacify one of her cravings this morning.

'Breakfast,' he said. 'Then you can choose where you wish to go today. *Si?*'

Her head jerked up where she stood, hastily zipping up her case, and he was smacked with the suspicion that the contents were something she'd rather he didn't see. Not that it mattered. By the time he was finished her every secret would be unearthed.

'Wow, Thane. Colour me surprised—you're giving me a *choice*?'

For now. '*Si*, of course. The first of many. Come and sit with me—let me feed you.'

As if she were an antelope and he a great ferocious lion, she approached him warily. Such an astute character, she was. Then he heard a canine sniff from behind him and accepted that he wasn't the only predator in the vicinity.

'Ah,' she said. 'Now I get why you were throwing sticks. Why are they smacking their lips as if I'm on the menu? Good Lord, they're huge. What *are* they?'

Slipping his arm around her waist, he tugged her to him and murmured in her ear. 'Rhodesian Ridgebacks. Maybe they find you as delicious as I do. Must be all those round American chocolatey…'

With a long-suffering sigh, she rolled her eyes and pushed past him. 'Yes, yes—all right, Romeo.'

All that feisty sass made him grin as he pulled out a chair and watched her sashay into the padded wicker seat.

'Thank you.'

Bending at the waist, he pressed his lips to the graceful slope of her bare shoulder and murmured, 'Welcome…' relishing both the shimmy that danced down her body *and* the way he'd already stripped her of that haughty veil.

He sank into the chair adjacent to hers and strove for nonchalance. 'I take it you spoke to your sister?' That he was ignorant of the whole conversation sat in his guts like a rock.

The sun bathed her in a warm glow, picking out the honeycomb strands in her hair, and she swept a stray tendril back from her temple in a decidedly nervous gesture. 'Yes. I told her I was staying with you for a couple of days.'

Thane didn't bother arguing that point. *Yet.*

'So, thank you for...' She shook her head, sending that wayward lock tumbling back over her face. 'Why on earth I'm *thanking* you for returning my own property to me, when it was originally your fault I lost it, is beyond me—but I do appreciate you sending for it.'

'You are most welcome. See? I am not so bad after all.'

'Oh, you are *very* bad, Thane. Of that I am in no doubt.'

A dark laugh erupted from his chest. 'Fortunately for me you like me that way. It turns you on.'

A blush that spoke more of pique than passion flurried across her cheeks, but her scathing retort perished as his man at the house—Pietro—appeared and laid a mound of homemade madeleines, croissants and cream-filled pastries on the table before her.

That serene breeding of hers came rushing to the fore. 'Everything smells delicious—thank you so much. Did you make these?'

Pietro fastened his warm hazel gaze on her. 'My wife, Your Royal Highness. But she will only cook for our Prince.'

Thane's good mood disintegrated and he clenched his teeth. It didn't matter how many times he told the man to call him Thane, he still got *our Prince*. Respectful, yes, but it shafted him with guilt—because despite his title his hands were largely tied, and if he'd played things differently he'd be in the position to do a damn sight more for them.

Luciana arched one brow in his direction. 'Why only Thane?'

'Eat, Luciana,' he ordered, knowing what was coming.

He didn't want Pietro's gratitude. It was Thane's job to procure him a better life. He was the one to blame for the mess they were in. If he'd been stronger, hidden his true ambitions better, his father would have given him the throne upon his death. Instead of passing it over to the power-hungry, greedy lech that was Franco Guerrero.

Naturally Luciana didn't take a blind bit of notice—*Dios*, she was an obstinate little thing—and she blinked up at Pietro with those gorgeous brandy eyes no man could possibly resist. Not even happily married Pietro, with his six girls and loose tongue.

'He gives us a home, our own land. No one but the crown owns land on Galancia, but Thane gives us acres of his vineyards and my family make the best wines on the island. Then he makes sure my girls can travel north, go to school. He fixes everything.'

'Pietro...don't. Please.'

Every time he heard those words it just reminded him of the thousands of others he couldn't help. Though now he had Luciana all that would change, wouldn't it? *Dios*, he couldn't wait. His patience shredded more by the day.

Luciana, whose only focus was Pietro, said, 'Oh, he does?'

As if some mental explosion had occurred in that ingenious brain of hers, so many emotions flickered across her exquisite face that he was hard-pressed to pick out one.

'*Si,*' Pietro said avidly. 'The best man to walk the earth. And now *you* are here, and everything will be—'

Thane glanced up to silence him. He didn't want these two days to be mired with talk of his throne. But, fisting his hand beneath the table, he warred with an internal battle to be forthright. At least with himself. Truth was, he wanted Luciana to want him. To choose *him* over Augustus. Not to feel pushed or obligated in any way. And he refused to read too deeply into that.

'Now I'm here...?' Luciana prompted.

Pietro grinned. 'He will be happy at last. All will be well.'

Guilt blanched her flawless skin and she composed a

spurious smile that made Thane uneasy. Made him doubly sure he was missing something.

'You must meet my wife. I will never have peace if she does not speak to you.'

Thane almost groaned aloud. They would be here all day and Luciana would be subjected to God knows what.

'Pietro? I don't think we have time. Luciana wishes to explore—isn't that right, angel?'

The wide-eyed gleam she launched his way was anything but angelic. It was positively devious and it made his blood hum. She wanted to hear more, he realised.

'We have plenty of time...*darling*.' She emphasised that endearment—the very one that made his heart lurch—with a swift kick to his shin as she peered up at the other man all guile and innocence. 'I think that's a wonderful idea, Pietro. I would love to meet her.'

Relishing Thane's discomfort, she flashed her teeth at him, all saccharine sweetness. The dark look he volleyed back said she would pay highly for it. Later.

Then again, Pietro had wandered off—so why wait?

Easing forward in his seat, he slid wicked fingers over the delicate curve of her knee beneath the table, then made small teasing circles as they ascended higher and higher up her inner thigh.

The light flush that coloured her cheeks made a gradual descent across her chest, down over her breasts, and the glass of freshly squeezed orange juice in her fist rippled as she clamped her thighs together, imprisoning his hand.

'See that knife?' she whispered in a rush, motioning to the lethal blade on the table-top. 'I won't hesitate to chop those fingers off.'

'Ah, you won't do that, Luciana.'

'I wouldn't be so sure, if I were you. Don't underestimate me, Romeo.'

Flipping his hand, he forcibly nudged her legs apart. 'While I have no intention of underestimating you, I believe you'll soon see sense. Because what will I pleasure you with then?'

Her breathing became short and shallow, making her deep cleavage taunt him with a subtle quivering heave, and he had the sinful urge to ramp up her erotic want higher still. So he stroked one finger over the lace of her panties and ran his tongue along his bottom lip suggestively.

'Actually…who needs fingers? I can think of various other ways to torment you.'

And he would use every one to lure her in. No matter what it took, by the weekend both Luciana and the throne would be his.

She was going to murder him. Wrap her hands around his throat and send him to meet his maker—the devil himself. That was if she didn't choke on the uncut testosterone in the air first. Arrogant and downright debauched—that was what he was.

She couldn't move or whimper a sound, since Pietro was still fiddling with a coffee pot at the far end of the deck—and of course the shameless reprobate just *loved* that…the possibility of them getting caught likely got him off. It certainly didn't excite *her* blood. A woman of her gentility and refinement should be appalled at his sybaritic behaviour. And she was. Utterly.

Squirming, she tried to dislodge his hand and alleviate the dark pulse that throbbed in her pelvis. She wanted them back on topic. Wanted to hear every word that *wasn't* being said. It was that stuff that interested her—far more than his wandering lasciviousness.

Liar.

She felt like an insect that had inadvertently strayed into a spider's web, her every move ensuring greater entrapment, but right now she didn't care. Entangled as she was, there was far more going on here than met the eye.

Pietro vanished around the corner and she smacked Thane's arm away as she spun on him, eyes narrowed.

'Your uncle runs Galancia in a dictatorship, does he not? No government, no parliament to speak for the people, all the power coming from the man at the top. The state owns every acre of land, therefore every piece of brick and mortar too.'

That did it.

He flung himself back in his seat, taking his wicked fingers with him. It was if he'd found a state of mindless pleasure and was put out at her stopping his fun. *Tough.*

'I am sure you know he does, *princesa*.'

'So by giving Pietro his own land you're breaking your own rules?'

He picked up his espresso and downed the treble shot. 'They are not mine.'

'No? Are you saying you don't agree with them?'

His nonchalant shrug belied the curious tension in his menacingly hard frame. 'I don't think it's fair that the people can't reap the benefits of their hard work, that's all.'

Fair? 'You're indirectly hinting at a democracy, Thane.'

'I might be.'

Shock made her rock back in her seat. The dark, dangerous, autocratic Prince of Galancia wanted a *democracy*? While Arunthia had been a democratic state for years, it was the last thing she'd expected here.

'Is this what you're planning to do when you rule?'

'I might be.'

Good Lord. 'And so you take from the rich to give to the poor in the meantime?'

He scratched his jaw lazily. 'On occasion. Or I may just have paid Pietro's family for building this house.'

'How much? Thirty million?'

'I'll have you know it's the going rate.'

'Is it *really*?'

This was unbelievable. Staggering. She'd been absolutely right. She had no idea who he was. And nor did anyone else.

Including her father. Which wasn't surprising. Since Thane didn't have overall control he naturally wanted to keep his true agenda firmly under wraps.

'Still being a hero, then, Thane?' she asked softly.

Just as he'd been when he'd saved her from a fate worse than death in Zurich. Just as he'd been when he'd appeared once again out of nowhere in Courchevel. As if she'd conjured him up. Like some freak happenstance or serendipity.

An assassin? A mercenary? *This* man? She doubted that very much.

But, oh, no, he really didn't like being called a hero. The angry glitter in his eyes told her that. He was a testament to leashed power, Luciana decided. No need to shout when he could incite a quake with one look or a word. So intense. And he was heart-thumpingly gorgeous with it.

'Quiet, Luciana. Or I will silence that mouth for you. *Again.* And don't think I won't.'

His dominant power pushed at her, hot and hard, and she blushed like a teenager with a crush.

'Oh. I believe you. But this time I'm not giving you the chance.' That was what had got her into this mess to start with.

She might be here against her will, or rather she'd had little choice, but the sliver of pride she had left was a precious commodity she could ill afford to lose. So there was no way she was falling for that again. She knew better. Kiss her once and he'd had her on a plane. Kiss her twice and she'd find herself bound for Outer Mongolia, or flat on her back on her way to a priest. Though why the man wanted to marry her specifically she couldn't begin to fathom.

Why can't you just accept he wants you for you, Luce?

Because that would be plain stupid.

He arched one of those devilish brows. 'You know better than to challenge me, Luciana.'

The dark promise in those words made her shiver. And if his obsidian eyes had seemed compelling before, now they were like magnets, pulling on the iron in her blood, making it race around her body.

Lifting her tall glass, she splashed some orange juice down her parched throat, relishing the tangy sweetness that burst over her tongue, determined to wrestle back her poise. *Get back on topic, for heaven's sake.*

'Anyway,' she said. 'Why build a home here? Don't get me wrong—it's absolutely stunning—but why not live at Galancia Castle?'

His gaze drifted out to sea, but not before she saw the shadow of pain wash over him. 'I live there too. But my uncle and I are not the best of housemates. Even with thousands upon thousands of square feet and over two hundred walls.'

Seemed to her they were divided in more ways than one. Even as she struggled to take it all in she dug for more. 'I've heard it's one of the most opulent, palatial castles in the world.'

'It is the devil's lair.' A deep feminine voice sounded from beside her. 'Our Prince is better here. That place makes him dark and that man drains the life from him. Welcome... *welcome.*'

Thane shoved his hands through his raven hair, discomfort and agitation leaching from him.

Luciana yearned to straddle his lap, take away his pain just as she'd once done, but instead she jiggled her chair backwards to welcome Pietro's wife.

'Buenos dias,' she said, standing to accept a warm greeting and a kiss to both cheeks. The astounding affection filled her heart with elation and almost thrust her into a stupor.

Cupping her face, the petite brunette spitfire beamed. 'Good gracious, you are a real beauty. Little wonder he will not take—'

'Hanna,' Thane ground out in warning.

'Ah, hush. Let an old woman be happy.' She clapped her palm over her chest. 'This will be the best Christmas we have ever seen.'

It took all of Luciana's willpower to maintain her serenity. Never mind that the woman had just told the dark Prince to hush—why the blazes was she casting her festive aspirations on Luciana? Why should she think Luciana would be here for Christmas? Was Thane so darn confident he'd been shouting it from the rooftops?

Of all the arrogant, conceited...

It was on the tip of her tongue to tell every Galancian within hearing distance that she'd be long gone by then. But as if Thane sensed her freefall he picked up her hand, lifting it to his lips. Tenderly he kissed the sensitive pulse-point that pounded at her inner wrist as he locked those mesmerising eyes on hers.

His electric energy zeroed in on her. The panicked dizziness abated. All extraneous noise drained from her perception until there was only him. Until she plunged back to her seat in a dreamlike daze.

How do you do this to me?

And then there was this couple, welcoming her with open arms despite the inbred hatred between Arunthians and Galancians, behaving as if she were their saviour. It was surreal. But it was wonderful too.

Even his beasts gazed at her with loving amber-hued puppy-dog eyes, one of them even resting its slavering chin on her knee. Lord, she couldn't resist his dogs. Had to stroke the short, furry wheat-brown coat. Brush those velvety ears between her thumb and forefinger.

Natanael would adore you, she thought with a stab of anguish.

He would adore all of this. He had pined and pleaded for a four-legged friend and he loved people, being the centre of their world. She could just hear him chattering, see him frolicking on the beach, dwarfed by these huge hounds, building sandcastles with Thane, his—

Luciana closed her eyes and swallowed thickly around the fear clotting her throat. She didn't want to make the connection—didn't want to acknowledge who this man was to her son. Had to focus on escaping, protecting Nate…

But what if in reality it wasn't Thane he needed protecting *from*? What if Thane was the only person in the entire world who could truly protect *Nate*?

He wasn't the man she'd met in Zurich. He was harder. More ruthless. More determined. And yet he wasn't the monster people claimed him to be.

Head pounding, as if it had been jammed in a nutcracker and split open, she couldn't think. Couldn't breathe.

So she smiled and nodded in all the right places while the endless waters of the Med called to her, the sound of its gentle lap, its tranquil stillness, soothing the disharmony in her heart and mind. But she didn't need to be looking at the ocean to realise she was burying her head in the sand. *Again*. That was exactly what she'd done in Hong Kong. Her utmost to pretend that her time wasn't running out. And where had it got her? Into inevitable torment when faced with reality.

If she waded through the mess of enemy nations and her throne she was a mother. First and foremost. Yes, if Natanael came to light it would ruin her in the eyes of her people and her father would likely disown her. But so be it. The only reason she'd kept him quiet was to keep him safe.

She'd pleaded to have him. The fact that he was alive right now was why she lived with the pain. The fact that his beautiful face lit up her entire world was why she lived in the dark. But if there were no danger to him there would be no reason for his true identity not to be known. His happiness was the most important thing to her. And if her little boy could have a daddy who was a good man—who would love him and protect him above all else—then Nate deserved that and so did Thane.

As for her crown… Her father would have to bend his rules and laws. Allow Claudia to take the throne despite the fact that Lucas wasn't of blue blood. Or he'd have to get over the fact he'd washed his hands of Andalina years ago and command her return from New York. Granted, the thought of Andie being Queen was hellishly scary, but her father would have no choice. If she was ruined, the damage was already done.

For the first time in years Luciana had choices. She only had to use them wisely. Be absolutely sure she was doing the right thing by telling Thane the truth.

Hanna and Pietro bade them a fond goodbye, leaving them alone once more.

'I believe I promised you a date,' he drawled. 'Lunch at the southern reef? A horse-ride along the beach or up into the vineyards? It's beautiful up there. What's your pleasure, angel?'

You. Heaven help me...you.

The man being worshipped by the sun before her. She wanted him to be real. Wanted the portentous voice inside her to be quiet, cease whispering that she was sitting in an audience watching a play—a performance being acted to perfection just for her—while she was blind to the true intent of the show.

'What do you want, Luciana?' he asked huskily.

A proper family. A wonderful daddy for Natanael. Love.
But all she said was, 'All of the above.'

CHAPTER EIGHT

IN HINDSIGHT, A horse-ride probably wasn't the greatest of ideas, considering he'd almost choked on his own tongue when Luciana had poured that luscious body into some lightweight fawn jodhpurs and a figure-hugging cerise pink T-shirt—the outfit borrowed from one of Pietro's rake-thin girls. Talk about an exercise in torture.

He'd just put in the longest twenty-minute car-ride of his life. And now he cursed the *idiota* who had secreted the royal stables so far inland. He would fire the man if he didn't suspect it had been himself.

Arms folded across his wide chest, his foul temper exacerbated further still when every stable boy tripped over himself to attend her, but eventually she chose a deep chestnut thoroughbred named Galileo and Thane took his favourite black stallion, Malvado. The twinkle in Luciana's eyes told him she thought 'wicked' a very apt name for his beast of a mount. He didn't bother arguing. It was true that only Thane could dominate him.

Unsurprisingly, she rode like a pro and lured him into a race up into the vineyards, with the rich earth spraying in their wake, the fresh breeze whipping her bronze hair behind her and slapping her cheeks with colour.

Never had she looked more bewitching or more free. More real and more like his Ana.

Gradually she slowed to a trot, then an easy walk, and Thane pulled at the reins and drew up beside her.

'Good?' he asked.

'Yes. Wonderful.'

Those pink-smothered breasts rose and fell with her every soft pant and a huge smile curved her lips. Lips he wanted to make love to until her breath was ragged for *him*.

'I didn't expect it to be so gorgeous here. Warmer than home for December.'

Thane felt the muscle in his jaw spasm as he ground his teeth hard. Galancia would soon be her home, and the sooner she accepted that the better for his state of mind.

'Then again, you are closer to Africa here,' she went on. 'The air is hot and sultry. Everything just feels…'

'Relaxed? Calm?'

'Exactly. Maybe too calm—like the calm before a storm.'

A pensive crease lined her brow and she threaded the leather reins in between her long fingers, staring far into the distance as if she were a million miles away. Much as she'd done at breakfast. It vexed him because he was blind to the reason. He wanted her *here*. With him.

'Penny for them?'

She fobbed him off with a rueful smile. 'I doubt they're worth that much.'

Thane didn't believe her for a second, but let it go when she lifted in her saddle to twist and take in their surroundings. The endless rows of vines were heavy with juicy red grapes and lush dark green foliage.

'So these are your famous vineyards? Never tried the wine myself.'

'You should. In fact tonight I'll pour you a glass of one of the best wines in the world.'

She arched one brow at the vainglory lacing his words but he gave a nonchalant shrug. Why shouldn't he be proud of what they'd achieved? And moreover…

'The northern terrain is home to our much-lauded olive groves too. Far better than yours.'

'Now, now, Thane. Your head is getting a little *too* big over there.'

He grinned, amazed that they were joking about what had once been a life-threatening issue.

'Once upon a time we grew the best oranges too. Arunthian oranges are tasteless in comparison.'

She rolled her eyes. 'Of course they are.'

'I'm serious. Our crops were said to be the best in Europe. But your great-grandfather didn't like it that overseas trade demand was greater for ours, or that we made more money than he did. So he sent in men to disease our crops. Not one survived.'

Her head reared as if he'd slapped her. 'That's a lie! Nothing more than propaganda!'

'It is not. I swear it. In many ways we continue to suffer from that loss now.'

'But…but that's terrible.'

'*Si.* It is. Just one of the spats our countries—or should I say the houses of Verbault and Guerrero—have engaged in over the centuries.'

Her nose scrunched up as she grimaced. 'Hard to believe we were allies—sister islands at one time. I have heard some gruesome and horrific accounts…'

'And I bet we were always the villains.'

Thane didn't bother to wait for her to agree; they both knew he was right.

'I won't lie—I imagine we committed many an outrageous act not to be proud of, but most were in retaliation. If you care to go back far enough it all comes down to Arunthia's greed. Galancia has always been the richer in industry, and many an Arunthian leader has tried to take it by force. Almost succeeded two or three times too. But it just made us stronger. Hence we have an indomitable military presence. Now no one would dare to touch us.'

Those decadently long lashes swept downward, as if his words weighed heavily on her mind. 'I can see why you wish to be feared, in that case. To protect what you have. No matter what it takes.'

Thane narrowed his gaze on her, sure there was a deeper meaning to her hushed words—which had been spoken in a cracked parody of her usual tone. When she failed to elucidate he ploughed on, riding the imperative desire for her to know. Understand.

'We stop at nothing. Which has caused a whole new set of problems for us. Because to protect, to build an army, takes an obscene amount of money. More than you could ever imagine. So the crown hoards the land for revenue and taxes businesses until they can't breathe—until we've suffocated our own. All to make us indestructible. More powerful than any other. While our children need new schools and our hospitals are in dire need of repair.'

Sadness crept over her demeanour, making her eyes darken. 'That makes so much sense it's scary.'

'My uncle will never release those bonds on our people. Nor will he let the feud go—just like my father before him. His father before that. The hatred is inbred.'

'I know. My father is the same. But what I don't understand is why Franco Guerrero is in power and you're not. Why haven't you taken your throne?'

'Must we talk about this now, Luciana?'

'Yes, Thane, we must. You brought me here against my wishes. You talk about marrying me…which is ludicrous. We don't even know one another. And basically all you expect me to go on is rumours and secrets and lies. So here I am blindfolded, smack-bang in the midst of a labyrinth, not knowing which way to turn. Can't you see that?'

Disquiet hummed through his mind. He didn't particularly want her to know how dark he was inside, how deeply twisted by it all.

They'd reached a shaded wrought-iron arbour often used by his workers and Thane swung his right leg over the saddle and dropped onto uneven ground, determined to tread carefully over the minefield that was the past.

He was too close to success to risk everything now, by admitting he'd been a trigger away from assassinating her father. Especially when some days he regretted not doing so, since his people had ultimately paid the price. Other days he accepted it would have severed the very last thread of humanity he'd been clinging to at the time. And today, looking at the man's daughter—the woman he wanted as his wife, the woman who would give him his crown—he couldn't help but wonder if fate truly did move in mysterious ways.

Vigilance tautened his striking features, telling Luciana she was trying to open a conversational door best left shut. Then an artful devious light shone in his dark eyes and he stretched out his arms, gripped her waist and lifted her down, dragging her body against his.

The friction charged her pulse and set off a chain reaction she was powerless against. Inside her bra her breasts grew heavy, aching to be touched. Those burning butterflies went wild, flitting in and around her ribcage, and her panties suddenly felt too damp, too tight.

'Let's have lunch in the shade,' he murmured, his voice enriched with sin. 'It's stifling out here in the open.'

Translation: *I'll seduce you in the bushes until you forget your own name, never mind this discussion.*

Er…*no*. She thought not.

Though her resolve would be less painful to stick to if she stopped gawping at the man. Thane in a pair of tall sepia leather boots, black riding trousers and a skin-tight red polo shirt—collar flicked up to tease his hair and short sleeves lovingly caressing his sculpted biceps—was a head-rush all on its own.

So she made a clumsy job of sidestepping outside his magnetic force field.

Out came his arm, to snake around her waist, and she

dodged like the netball champion she'd once been and shook her head. 'Oh, no, you don't. I know full well what you're up to, Romeo, and you can forget it. *Talk.*'

Growling, he turned away. 'Fine.'

Then, just as she breathed a sigh of relief, he came at her from another angle, as if he'd played her with misdirection and now...*pounce*...stole a tummy-flipping, bone-liquefying kiss from her mouth. Only to grin with acute smugness and walk away.

Her hand shot out and she found Galileo, to steady herself, even as she bit her lip to stifle a gurgle of laughter. He was incorrigible. Couldn't stand being told no. Losing in any way. And, seriously, she shouldn't laugh—because the man was dangerous with it. Kidnapping, stealing kisses... He was off-the-charts unpredictable, and that scared her more than anything.

And it thrills you just as much.

Thane grabbed the lunch bag and Luciana rolled a blanket across the grass beneath the leafy trellised ceiling, where it was blissfully cooler. Then she sat cross-legged and unpacked a tapas feast of cold cut meats, cheeses and rosemary-scented bread.

Throat dry, she drank greedily from a bottle of sparkling water, trying not to splutter or drool as Thane dropped to the red chequered blanket and lounged back on his elbows in an insolent pose, crossing one ankle over the other. She had the shameless urge to climb over his lap, sit on those muscular thighs and feel all that latent erotic power beneath her. And—just her rotten luck—he caught her staring and fired her the most indecently hedonistic smile she'd ever seen.

Luciana deflected his corruption tactics with a haughty sniff. 'I'm waiting. So talk.'

'I have the strangest urge to take you over my knee.'

She harnessed the shiver that threatened to rattle her spine. 'And *I* have the strangest urge to get back on that horse and leave you to eat lunch by yourself.'

The brute actually grinned at that, then popped an olive in his mouth. Though when his humour faded, to be replaced by an aching torment, she almost let him off the hook, hating to see him in the throes of anguish. Oh, he banked it soon enough—but it was too late.

'When my father knew he was dying I had only just turned seventeen...' He paused, as if figuring out his next words. 'He ordered me to do a job, and at the very last moment I defied him. I thought I'd seen and felt his fury before then. I had seen nothing.' He shrugged blithely. 'I deserved every blow for going against him, and I could have lived with that, or anything else he doled out to me personally. What I hadn't expected was the depth of his wrath and the price my people would pay.'

Abruptly, he jerked upright and rested his forearm on one bended knee.

'When I failed him he decided I was too cocky, too young...too free-thinking to rule. Too liberal. I had shown my true colours. My father and my uncle are of the same ilk. Dictators. Born and bred militia. So my punishment was a stipulation that said I couldn't take power until I was thirty years old. Until I had learned my lesson.'

Outrage and the fiercest taste of bitter acrimony roiled in her stomach. To give his uncle time to work him over, no doubt. As if *anyone* could reshape Thane's mind. The very idea was ludicrous.

'I deserved every blow...'

The man didn't even flinch or care that he'd been beaten. No, all he cared about was that he'd failed his people.

'What made you break from the pack?' she asked, awed. 'Being of the same ilk and all.'

Luciana couldn't begin to comprehend the strength it would have taken to set himself apart from such men. The stories she'd heard—the ones she had nightmares about, imagining Natanael embroiled in them—brought her out in a cold sweat.

In one graceful movement he was up on his feet, leaning against an iron post, focused on the rolling hills.

'My mother, I think. It was her dream, and she used to talk about how her family would pray morning, noon and night for a better tomorrow. A tomorrow when the people could speak for themselves, have a say in how they lived. A day when they owned their own lands and could reap the benefits of what they sowed. When people's lives would be that much richer and more fulfilling if they were given the chance to aspire.'

Heaviness encroached on her chest at the grief painting his words blue. 'She sounds like she was a wonderful woman, Thane.'

Luciana knew he'd lost her young. And if the stories were true and his mother had been taken, stolen from her loved ones, his childhood must have been a war zone in more ways than one.

'A tortured soul is a more apt description.'

She could hear the dark resonance of his painful past echo through him, distorting his voice, and her eyes flared as he grabbed hold of a tangled vine from above and ripped it down, its thorns spearing into his palm. Within seconds blood dripped from his fist.

Luciana scrambled to her feet. 'Thane...?'

His eyes were the blackest she'd ever seen, and she realised he wasn't even aware he'd hurt himself. Panic punched her heart.

'Don't do that, *querido*. Look what you're doing. Thane? *Thane*!'

He blinked, over and over, refocusing on her. 'Sorry, angel, what is it?'

'G...Give me your hand.' She pulled a handkerchief from her pocket and wrapped the white cotton round his palm, biting her lip when deep red stained the cloth.

Thane searched her face with a confounded expression,

as if no one had ever cared enough before to stop him hurting. And that made her aching heart weep for him.

Pointing up to the small scar on his chin, she asked softly, 'Did that hurt when you did it?'

'I can't remember. I do not think so.'

Good Lord, his pain threshold had to be off the charts.

'When did you do it?'

'This one?'

Up came his hand and he rubbed over the thin white line with one fingertip.

A fresh stab of wretchedness almost struck her down. It was just like when Nate talked about falling out of the blossom tree at their apartment near Hong Kong. He would touch the scar on his arm when he recalled it. The likeness in mannerism was uncanny—and so bittersweet.

'I was twelve, I think. I'd dropped a thirty-five-millimetre and shattered the casing.' He smiled and shook his head ruefully. 'Let's just say I never once fumbled with the damn thing again.'

'Twelve? And he punished you? He beat you for…?' She swallowed thickly. 'How could he *do* that?'

He shrugged off her empathy. 'It's not an issue. I was born to rule, just as he was. Raised to defend, not to feel. A honed weapon. He did what he had to do. Probably what had been done to him. I accept that.'

'No. *No*, Thane. No child should have to accept that. Don't you *dare* accept that. He didn't have to be brutal or so cruel. Are you saying because you were raised like that you would do that to your children? Your son?'

Snatching his hand away, he stepped back as if she'd physically backhanded him. Anger, affront and hurt flooded the space between them. 'How could you think me capable of that, Luciana?'

Oh, God, she'd had nightmares about exactly that. As her father had filled her head with tales—and yes, okay, some facts too—she'd fought her own instincts. Scared witless, out of her mind. Missing him so badly she couldn't eat or sleep or breathe without hurting. So she'd written letters. What seemed like hundreds of letters. Only to burn them.

Tears splashed up behind her eyes. She couldn't stop them. And he didn't like it—not one bit.

Panic laced his voice. 'Luciana, what is wrong?'

'I'm sorry,' she whispered. 'I'm so sorry.'

His riveting handsome face creased with confusion. 'Why? Why are you sorry?'

Shaking her head, she forced a smile. She knew it wept with sorrow and dejection, so she made it brighter. Smoothed the damp hair from his brow.

'Do you feel *me* when I touch you?' she asked.

'You're about the only thing in the world I do feel, Luciana.'

Oh, God.

Out of control—as always with this man—she reached up in search of his mouth. Desperate to take his pain away. To take hers with it too. Because she now knew what she had to do and it would likely destroy them. Destroy this. Destroy any chance of happiness they would ever have.

As she lifted up on her tiptoes he surged downwards, closing the gap, pressing a frantic kiss to her lips.

She reached up and grabbed handfuls of his shirt, feeling the flex of his hard muscle beneath her fingertips. One kiss, she promised herself. Just one kiss so she could feel his lust and affection. Surely it would be enough to last? It would have to be enough.

Thane's fingers speared into the heavy fall of her hair, cradling her nape, his grip fierce and exquisitely firm, and with one long, languorous flick and thrust of his tongue into her mouth her knees buckled underneath her.

His cat-like reflexes kicked in and he dropped his hands to her waist to keep her upright.

'*Dios*, I crave you like a physical ache. Not here, though, angel. I can't lose it with you here,' he breathed in a rush of warm air over her cheek as he ran his nose up the side of hers and rested there for a gloriously intimate beat.

No. She couldn't possibly sleep with him. It would make everything a hundred times worse. And what was more…

'Thane, you have to stop calling me that, okay?' It tore off another piece of her heart every time he did.

'What…? Angel? Why? It's what you reminded me of last night in the limousine, with your hair this colour. Darkly spun gold. Seraphic. Beautiful. As *you* are, Luciana. Inside and out.'

'D…Don't put me on a pedestal, Thane. I'm no angel. Sooner or later I'll drop from a great height.'

And, like finely spun glass, she would shatter to the floor in a million pieces.

A rueful light flickered in his eyes as he hiked one broad shoulder. 'Then maybe we will be equal.'

Guilt. So much guilt it seemed to suffocate his soul.

'What your father did—giving control to your uncle— it's not your fault.'

Scepticism vied with his obvious desire to believe her.

'What job or mission did you refuse to do, anyway? What would anger him so much that he'd delay your taking the throne for so long?'

That had to have been ten years ago…

A shadow swarmed over his face and in that moment somehow she *knew*.

Foreboding crackled down her spine and she stumbled back a step. 'Go on. Say it.'

He shoved his hands through his wind-tousled raven-black hair and his chest swelled as he hauled in air. 'How did you know?'

'I wasn't sure until right this moment. But rumours have a way of reaching the right ears and poisoning minds.'

A muscle ticked in his jaw as he gave a short nod. 'I disobeyed a direct order and refused to kill your father.'

CHAPTER NINE

LUCIANA CURLED UP on a cushioned recliner on the beach and gazed up at the midnight sky, wishing on a billion twinkling diamond stars that Thane's business calls would take all night. But, as she already knew, burying her head in the sand would help no one—least of all herself.

The drive back down to the coast had been taut with tension, and by the time dinner had been served on the upper floor balcony Luciana had been strung so tightly she'd barely eaten one mouthful of the delicious seafood paella Hanna had slaved over. Which had only made her feel guiltier still. And she wouldn't have thought that was possible.

Closing her eyes, she recalled their brief conversation in the car.

'I didn't want to tell you,' he'd said. 'I thought you'd hold it against me.'

'I'm glad you told me. You saved his life in the end. It must have been a horrendously hard call for you. Thank you...'

Thane had saved her father's life. Paid an extortionate price for disobeying his tyrannical King. All for a man he hated. His enemy.

And how is he being repaid? His son is being kept from him. I didn't know. I didn't know any of this.

The guilt and pain tearing through her in one relentless lash after another wouldn't cease. Not for a second.

One day. She'd been here one day and the enormity of

what she'd discovered had her reeling. In truth, she wasn't sure she was taking it all in.

The rush of the ocean lapping over the shore was broken by the sound of bare feet padding down the deck, sending her heart trampolining to her throat and her stomach vaulting with a hectic tumble of dread and anticipation.

Thane straddled the recliner in front of her, one long-stemmed glass of ruby-red liquid in his large grip.

With a wriggle, she edged back to give his broad frame more room, and rested her head against the mocha cushion to drink him in.

He was breathtaking. His dark, fathomless eyes pulled at her like a hypnotic suggestion pressing against her mind. A constant murmur of want that was becoming impossible to ignore. But fight it she would.

'You are very quiet since we got back,' he said, his voice low and warm with concern.

'Just thinking.'

'No more thinking of the past tonight, hmm? Let's focus on the future. On us.'

She wasn't sanguine enough to believe there would be an 'us' come the dawn.

You don't know that for sure, Luce. He might listen to you. Try to understand.

It was a sliver of hope she clung to.

Raising her arm, she brushed his hair back from his gorgeous face and his decadent sable lashes fluttered as if weighted in bliss, as if he adored her touch. It broke her heart.

'Relax, Luciana. You seem brittle enough to shatter.'

Smooth as silk, his voice caressed her skin—a tangible touch of his magnetic heat and power that lulled her to calm.

'Here—take a taste.'

Glancing at the glass of red wine he'd promised earlier, she tried to swallow past her raw, swollen throat. Heavens, no. Thane was intoxicating enough. Half a glass and she'd be the centrefold in the tawdriest scenario her imagination could conjure up.

'I don't think that's such a good idea, Thane.'

Truly, she was way out of her depth, lying here as he towered above her, dominating her world. Thane on a sensual mission was a demonic tidal wave to be reckoned with. But she wasn't convinced sleeping with him would do either of them any favours in the long run.

Still, the yearning pushed at her soul. Stronger in force since the revelations of the afternoon. *'You're about the only thing in the world I do feel...'* That must be why he'd brought her here. Right? She made him feel and he was chasing it. Why else would he go to the lengths he had? And more than anything she wanted to bring him pleasure in any way she could.

Those devastating eyes fixed on her as he swirled the wine around the crystal, giving it air, then took a sip before dipping one of his sinfully adroit fingers into the ruby depths.

Memories of the debauched passion those hands could wreak made the briny ocean breeze stutter in her lungs and she panted out, 'Thane...I think maybe I should turn in for the night. I'm tired and I...'

I'm petrified I will give in, and it would be so reckless, so stupid, no matter how much we both want it.

She inhaled deeply, grappling for strength, only to be drugged by his dark, delicious scent. It infused her lust-addled mind and corrupted her veins. It blazed a firestorm through her midriff that eventually simmered low in her abdomen in a searing burn.

Venturing to eradicate that hot, dark pulse at her core, she squirmed to sit upright in the recliner. 'Thane...I should go to bed.'

By morning she'd have figured out what to do. What to say. How to explain.

'I—'

'Do you think I don't know what I do to you, Luciana? Do you think I can't hear and see your body crying out for mine? Stop fighting this, angel. It's inevitable.'

Claret drizzled down his finger in red droplets as he reached up and painted her lips with the lusty juice, let the rich flavour flow over her tongue, where it blossomed into an ecstasy of ripened grapes, aged wood and sunlight.

With a whimper she flicked her tongue over the very tip and sucked it into her mouth, loving the underlying saltiness and texture of his skin.

A feral groan ripped past his throat and he stared at her glistening lips, where her tongue swirled around his finger... Then he whipped it out, swooped down and captured her mouth in an erotic devouring kiss.

Push him away, Luce. Do it now...

Can't. Impossible.

Luciana laced her fingers through his hair, fisting tight so he couldn't escape, and slanted her mouth over his, licking between his lips, duelling with the sinful lash of his tongue in total surrender.

She'd missed this so much. Kissing. Being held close. The amazing feeling of intimacy with a man—*her* man. Being a sensual woman, someone who was desired. Cosseted. Craved with a burning urgency that rendered her almost weak. It was heady and powerful and she'd missed it.

The robust richness of the wine blended with the potent dominant piquancy that was uniquely Thane—something that exuded vice and sin and seduction—and annihilated her every thought until she was trapped, entangled in his wicked snare.

They tore apart to breathe and yet he never stopped the cherishing ardour, only brushed kisses along her jaw and down her neck in a slow, wet slide that made her shiver and arch in a sinuous serpentine wave beneath him. Begging for his touch. Which he gave by brushing his knuckles down over her breast, teasing her nipple into a stiff peak.

Her wanton moan rent the air, and in reward he rained kisses over her cleavage where it spilled over the top of her low-cut dress. She pressed him in close to her, never wanting to let him go.

'I want you writhing for me, Luciana.'

His hot breath gushed over her skin.

'I want to make love to you, feel you cling to me, hear you beg for release. And then I'll hold you and kiss you in the dark, watch you fall asleep. Only to wake you by sliding down your body and devouring you with my mouth.'

Her lower abdomen clenched and turned achingly heavy, dampening her panties with wet warmth. And she wrapped her legs around his waist to grind against his thick erection in a silent plea for him to do all of that and more.

Gyrating, he ground back against her with long, animalistic groans. 'Just…' He scraped his teeth over the throbbing vein in her neck. 'Just make me feel again, Luce. Please.'

Oh, God. *You're about the only thing in the world I do feel…'*

The last wave of doubt drifted away as a tide of longing swept over her. To give him pleasure where she could. To take his pain away while he'd allow her to.

Cupping his jaw, she lifted his head to meet her gaze.

'I've missed you,' she whispered.

It was a shockingly dangerous thing to confess, because it left her so exposed and vulnerable. But in that moment the need for him to know how deeply she felt outweighed any sense of self-preservation she had left.

He eased back, his brow creased as he studied her face. 'Truth?'

'Absolute truth. I've missed you so much. So much I ached with it.'

Ah, Luce, you never had a hope of resisting him. Of keeping your heart locked away.

Farther back he moved, withdrawing from her, and her

stomach hollowed. Mind twisting, she wondered why he vibrated with rancour. And his touch...

He stroked up her thigh, burrowing beneath her floaty blush-pink sundress, his touch riding the line between pleasure and pain as if he were in the throes of anger. Suspecting she lied. His other hand roamed the curve of her waist, slid up to her midriff, where his thumb brushed the heavy underswell of her breast.

'You've missed me?' he said, flat and cool. 'Yet how many men have touched this body since I took it, Luciana? Since I made you mine?'

Staring into his turbulent eyes, she shook her head gently. 'Only you, Thane. There has only *ever* been you.'

Bizarre as it sounded, even to her own mind, she watched his barriers crumble and fall before her. Saw the floodgates to his emotions flung wide and time reversed. They stood still in the past. And there she was—his only focus, his entire world, the moon and the stars beyond. As if everything she'd convinced herself had been merely a dream was now a thrilling, breathtaking verity for her eyes only.

Her heart cracked wide open and she knew he could take it from where it lay, weak and defenceless outside her chest.

'Luciana, I...'

He cupped her face and she could feel his hands tremble as he rubbed his nose alongside hers, faltering, as if he feared what he truly wanted to say.

Instead he murmured against her lips, 'I...I need you.'

'Have me,' she choked out. 'Take me. However you want.'

One night was all they were likely to have and she would give him everything he desired. Everything in her power to give.

Tenderly he pressed his mouth to hers, then slanted his head and thrust his tongue into her mouth in a slow, languorous lick.

Luciana parried right back, glorying in his devout advance and retreat, the touch of his tongue against hers, as he took them both to passionate heights. And higher still into oblivion as he rucked her dress up and broke their lip-lock to tear it from her body. His hands were suddenly everywhere and nowhere. Big and clever, strong and capable hands. Leaving a trail of rapture in their wake.

She trembled all the while and let loose a pleading sob. 'Thane…I want you.'

'You have me, angel.'

'I want you naked. I want to feel you.'

He smiled wickedly as he stood tall, framed by the moon-lit ripple of the ocean like a bronzed demigod. 'You always did,' he said, his voice raspy with lust.

The back of her head dug into the cushion as she craned her neck to stare up at him. Unable and unwilling to look anywhere else as inch by delectable inch his burnished skin was revealed.

Thane grabbed the hem of his T-shirt and with a sleek twist of his mighty fine torso, ripped it up and over his head.

Luciana had to slick her dry lips at the sight of his arms stretched high, thick with muscle and threaded with veins. The sculpted perfection of his ripped chest, the ridges of his twelve-pack and the sweat-slicked super-sexy V of muscle on his pelvis. The arrow that teased and tormented its way down to the thick ridge that burst past the waistband of his low-slung board shorts.

She wanted them off too.

His long fingers went to the fastening and he cocked one brow, faltering—*no*, teasing, tormenting until her heart beat in her throat, thump-thump-thumping in excitement and exhilaration. Waiting. Wanting.

He unpopped the button. Excruciatingly slow.

Her impatience spiked. Two could play at that game.

She unclipped the front of her bra, but held it closed.

He growled.

She smiled.

And then he shoved the material down his densely corded legs.

Oh, wow.

Lord, she'd forgotten how big the man was. Thane—naked in all his rock-hard, battle-honed glory, frosted by moonlight—was a mind-bending orgasmic pleasure all on its own.

'You like, angel?'

'I absolutely *love*,' she breathed. 'Far more than any angel ever should.'

His dark eyes zeroed in on the lacy confection veiling her breasts, which were rising and falling under her laboured breathing, and he dropped back to the chair and unwrapped her as if she were a precious, delectable gift, slowly tugging the lace free. Then with splayed hands he smoothed down her midriff, watching, enraptured, as her flesh shimmied and pimpled in delight.

He'd always used to look at her that way. Fascinated. Glorying in what he could do to her. Just as his restraint had always evaporated when he reached the satin that shrouded the tight curve of her femininity, sending her torn panties somewhere over his left shoulder.

'This is better,' he rasped thickly, leaning down, closing in, teasing his tongue along her bottom lip. 'Much better.'

Possessive and heated and bruising in his intensity, he ravished her mouth, her throat, winding his way down to where he moulded her breast and thumbed her tight nipple. And when his tongue glossed over the plum-coloured peak her sex clenched around thin air, desperate for him to fill the aching void she'd languished in for years.

Arousal at fever-pitch, she hooked her legs around his back and ground against the erection that lay snug over her folds, the sinuous movement pulling a deep groan from his chest and making him suck harder, drawing the tight bud into his mouth. The responding tug in her core ripped an inarticulate cry from her throat.

'*Thane...*'

Feverish, she felt her pulse rocketing into the stratosphere and...*heck,* she was seconds away from hyperventilating. Had to remind herself to breathe.

'Patience, Luciana,' he growled, coercing her legs wide, lifting one up and over the chair-arm, then the other, until she was splayed for his depraved enjoyment.

'I'm going to kiss you until you can't breathe,' he said as he nuzzled down her stomach, grazing her skin with a day's growth of stubble and glancing up to meet her eyes through the sable fringe of his lashes. 'Lick you everywhere. Touch you everywhere. And you, Luciana, are going to lie there and *take it.*'

Oh, *yes.*

He crawled backwards, like the sleek, rapacious predator he was, dipping his head to drop a hot, open-mouthed kiss to each of her inner thighs. Luciana moaned and lifted her arms above her head to grip the top rail of the chair. Knowing he was about to blow her sky-high. Just the sight of his dark head bent, the feel of his hot breath teasing her throbbing sex, already pushed her to the brink.

'Oh, God, Thane. Come on—do it, *please.*'

She was sure he laughed. The callous brute. Though he did make up for it by parting her and raking over her folds, lavishing her with the velvet stroke of his hot tongue. He blew against her, then lashed his tongue once more.

'You're so aroused, angel. I forgot how sweet you taste— like honey. I could eat you alive, Luciana.'

She whimpered in shameless pleasure and thrust her hips in a rhythm that matched his tongue. He found her nub unerringly, sucking it into his mouth, and the cords of erotic tension inside her pulled tighter and tighter, until she was a boneless, quivering mass of desire.

'Thane. I can't...hold...on...'

She gasped for air. Then cried out when he pushed two thick fingers deep inside her saturated channel and stroked her to a splintering crescendo so magnificent her mind blanked with sensory overload.

Every muscle in her body stiffened and seized for one, two, three beats of her heart—then she exploded. Screamed as hot, hard sexual pleasure short-circuited her every nerve, shocking her into ecstasy so powerful she levitated off the lounger...suspended on an erotic plane, eyes locked on the midnight sky, the stars glittering above her...then literally slammed back to earth.

When she roused herself from delirium he was leaning above her and her heart fisted. She adored the way his damp hair hung around his face, making him look wicked. A perfect picture of debauchery.

He licked his lips and let rip a feral growl that seemed to come from the depths of his chest. 'I'm going to take you, Luciana. Fill you up. Pour myself into you. But I'll be damned if I'll do it on a beach. I want you in my bed.'

He lifted her up effortlessly and she wrapped her legs around his waist as he strode up the deck into his bedroom, kissing her all the while, never leaving her mouth even when they tumbled onto the bed, hands everywhere as they desperately tried to touch as much of each other as they could reach.

She tore her lips from his. 'Thane, please. Don't make me wait.'

Pushing his arms beneath her shoulders, he cupped her head in his hands, pinning her completely as he trapped her in his dark hypnotic gaze. 'You're mine, Luciana. You've always been mine.'

And then he pushed inside her in one long, deliciously hard thrust.

The stupendous clash of their cries filled the air, caromed off the walls.

Lord, the relief. The screaming, delirious relief and joy and rightness. The inordinate power they created was so all-consuming she slipped into that boneless delirious state once more.

Every one of her senses was as sharp as a pin and yet the moment was dreamlike. Even the erratic rhythm of his breathing seemed in perfect tandem to the thrash of her own heart.

Thane crushed her to him, cradling her, still embedded deep, his strong, muscular body shaking, his face buried in her neck. '*Dios*, Luciana. You feel so snug. So incredible...'

As if being inside her, reuniting their exquisite connection, had doused some of the urgency, deeper emotion now flooded the space between them, and Thane lifted his head and tenderly brushed her damp hair from her face, kissed her cheeks, her nose, her brow. So lovingly, so affectionately, that her heart splintered.

Too much, Luce, this is all too much. Back off or you won't survive this. Him.

No. She couldn't let go. Not yet.

His touch sculpted her behind, hooked around her thigh and urged it to curl over his hip as his pelvis locked with hers.

'That's it, angel, now let me watch you.'

He ground against her, watching, as if taking in every nuance of her feverish response, and when he hit her sweet spot she shivered and cried out, gripping his hair. He exploited it, rolling his hips, pushing his iron-hard length deep inside her, thrusting over and over until she was mindless, begging, delirious beneath him.

'*Thane...*'

Bliss opened up before her, fathoms deep, a chasm that would take her—body and soul. For one shimmering, breathless moment she teetered on the brink...and then she was falling, falling, tumbling, crashing as she hurtled towards ecstasy.

Thane picked up the pace, slamming into her, chasing his own nirvana, until he stiffened with a guttural cry of release, pouring himself inside her, racked with convulsions that left him weak and heavy in her arms. Trembling with the aftershocks like tiny flashes of lightning as the storm dissipated. And she loved it. Revelled in his weight, in his ragged breath whispering over the sensitive skin beneath her ear, his pounding heart against hers.

When lucidity fully returned she realised silent tears were tracking down the sides of her face. She saw again the Rhine Falls of Zurich—a stoic, bittersweet witness to her fragile joy. Because it didn't matter how tightly Thane wrapped her in his arms, as if she was all he'd ever wanted. As if she truly were his angel and they basked in the heavens. Because come the dawn all hell would break loose.

Luciana wrapped herself in a robe—the black silk her only armour and sat at the base of the bed, leaning against the carved footboard, watching the morning sun dapple over the hard contours of the man who lay sleeping, naked, on his stomach.

He was a study in masculine perfection. So beautiful. His face reminded her with exquisite poignancy of Natanael. And for the first time she didn't look at him and feel fear or trepidation or anger or dismay. She looked at him with one crystal-clear thought. Or rather she allowed herself to.

This was the man who had given her the son she loved so much. This was the man who'd helped to create a miracle of joy and wonder and beauty.

This man was the father of her child. The very man she'd fallen in love with so long ago. And she could not, *would* not keep their son from that man a moment longer. No more than she could keep Thane from Natanael.

And that man would not cast her out or take Nate from her. He would protect them both always. Even through his anger and rage. And, darn it, she would be strong through this. As lion-hearted and courageous as he was.

Satin shifted across the sumptuous mattress as he stretched and smouldered in all his abeyant heat. Her gaze locked on the muscles in his back, on the flex and bunch of his ruthless power.

Luciana fisted the folds of the robe at her neck, ordering herself not to reach out. To touch. Become lost in him all over again.

He prised his eyes open and smiled sleepily at her. Lord, it *hurt*.

'Come back up here, Luce. Let me hold you.'

She inhaled a lungful of fortifying air.

Come on, you can do this.

'I…I can't, Thane. I have to go home today. I have to go back to Arunthia and I need you to take me—like you promised.'

He sat up in one lithe rippling movement, like a panther uncurling, and pushed his tousled air back from his forehead. 'No, Luciana, don't say that.' His husky, lethargic voice grew stronger, firmer. 'You belong here with me. There's no reason for you to go back.'

Luciana swallowed around the searing burn in her throat. 'But there is, Thane. Someone is there that I can't leave. *Ever.*'

His expression darkened and she felt a frisson of fear. Flinched when he suddenly ripped the sheet from his body, vaulted from the bed and shoved his legs into a pair of black silk lounge trousers.

Hands on his hips, he spun on her. 'You love this person?'

'Yes,' she said, her voice cracking under pressure. 'I love him more than life itself.'

His eyes grew furious, dark as rain-laden thunderclouds. And she knew it was only going to get worse. This, she realised, was merely the beginning. God help her.

'Who do you love?' he demanded.

You can do this, Luciana. For him—for Natanael. Thane will rip your heart from your chest but this is not about you. It is about the little boy you love and his father. You are doing it for them. They deserve this from you. Do it. Do it.

'Please don't hate me, Thane,' she whispered, begging him. 'I was only trying to do the right thing. I was scared. I only wanted him to be safe—'

His beauty took on a terrifying, dangerous edge. 'Who, Luciana?' He flung his arms wide. 'Who do you love?'

'Your son. *Our* son.'

CHAPTER TEN

THANE'S PULSE ROCKETED and the room took an untimely spin, making his breath whoosh past his lips in a sickening rush.

'You...you had my child? I have a son?'

He couldn't have heard her correctly, he assured himself. But her beautiful brandy eyes filled to the brim and one drop escaped, glistened as it fell. Shimmered over her pink-washed cheeks, along the side of her nose and down to the corner of her full mouth.

A mouth that whispered, 'Yes...'

Thane shook his head jerkily. No. He could *not* be hearing her right. He would know. If he had a son he would know. Yet her words wouldn't stop ricocheting around his mind.

'You were pregnant?'

'Yes.'

'How?' he asked stupidly, feeling adrift and as vulnerable as the boy he'd once been. Trembling inside, feeling weak. He loathed it.

Luciana blinked, her brow pinching, her voice so small she appeared just as lost as he. 'Do you mean which time? I was on contraceptives, so I don't know. There were...'

So many times? Yes, there had been.

And they had made a baby. Together. His child. His *son*.

Then—*then* it hit. Like a bullet ripping through his chest. And it tore his world apart.

He jabbed his fingers through his hair and fisted the silky

strands. 'How does no one know my son exists, Luciana? How do *I* not know my son exists?'

'I fought to have him. I went away to have him. I—'

Acid flushed through his stomach and surged up to his throat. 'Ah, so he is your dirty little secret? My son. With Galancian blue blood. The man who will take my throne. He is *your dirty little secret*?'

Affront clawed inside his chest with merciless razor-sharp talons and he slammed his hand over his bare ribs to rub, to try and ease the gashes of pain tearing through him.

With an unsteady hand she reached out imploringly. 'I made a pact to have him. To keep him. I went to Hong Kong, where we were safe…'

'*Safe?* You kept his identity secret to keep him safe? Safe from *who*?' he hollered.

He didn't understand this. Any of it.

A sob racked her frame and she covered her mouth with one hand, fingers quivering over her lips. Lips bruised red and swollen from his kisses.

Dios, he had just made love to a deceitful, dishonourable bitch. He had just been embedded inside a liar and a thief. The woman who had stolen his son. Who *did* such a thing?

She's an Arunthian, Thane, what did you expect?

His brain was working so fast his thoughts tripped over themselves before he could even process the last.

'No one ever asked? *Suspected*?' he asked, dark incredulity pouring from his tone.

Sitting at the base of the bed, she bent her knees and wrapped her arms around them, curling that incredible hateful body into a defensive ball.

'No. We had a nanny—Crista—who has a son of her own. Very few other staff. I wanted him to have a normal childhood. A free life without the constraints of the crown. Without being suffocated by duty—'

Thane flung his arms wide. 'Yet you take away his rights

as a born royal! Why didn't you tell me? Were you *ever* going to tell me I had a son?'

Dios, he had a son. Maybe if he kept repeating the words it would sink in.

'I tried. So many times. I wrote letters—so many. I burned them. We didn't really know each other, Thane— you didn't even know my true identity.'

With the tips of her fingers she rubbed the moisture from the tender skin beneath her eyes and took a deep breath.

'Our countries are enemies—you know this. Only yesterday you admitted you almost assassinated my father. He knew, Thane. He *knew* it was you. I was so scared. And the rumours, the horrors I'd heard of this place—they chilled me. Your childhood…' She rocked a little, as if the mere thought of his youth pained her. 'The fact that you're staunch militia…raised for war, for fighting. I couldn't bear the thought of him being raised like that. Getting hurt. I still can't.'

She looked up at him through the veil of her lashes, those huge eyes pleading. Thane had to stiffen himself against their power.

'Please try to understand. I didn't even know you and your uncle were divided. I just—'

'Stop. Just *stop*.'

He couldn't abide her voice any more. Because it was becoming increasingly clear that the person she'd been trying to protect their son from was *him*. The only woman he'd ever let past his shields, the only woman he'd wanted to live his life with, thought him so monstrous that she'd feared for their son's life. And that almost killed him right where he stood.

'I cannot bear to hear your excuses any longer. Where is he? *Where* is my son?'

'At…at home—'

He sliced her off with a razored slash of his hand through the air. 'No, Luciana. He is not at home. His home is here— with *me*.'

Unable even to look at her, he pulled on his T-shirt and

bounded out onto the deck. Oblivious to where he was going.
Blind to what he was doing.

He felt vile. That ever-present blackness was rising like
a demonic tide inside him, swirling like a toxic storm. He
despised it. Despised *her* for causing it. Would do anything
to stop feeling—*anything*. And she'd done that too. Torn
down the walls that had barricaded his emotions, leaving
him defenceless, only to stab him in the back.

He brought his hand up in front of his face, watched his
flesh tremble and gritted his teeth as he balled it savagely
until his knuckles and wrist cracked and his strength began
to return. Until his heart was black and his blood ran cold.
Then he spun on his heels to stride across the patio.

'Thane, *wait*. Where are you going?'

That was one thing he *did* know.

'To get my son.'

A flash of memory arrowed through his mind and he
crashed to a halt. Turned with lethal calm to see her climb
from the bed and stand tall on those amazing legs—such
works of art. He'd had them wrapped around his waist as
he'd taken her against the shower wall, not two hours ago,
and it sickened him.

'The photograph I saw. Of you pushing a young boy on
a swing. In a park. When you were in China. He had ebony
hair just like mine...'

Dios, he'd been staring at a picture of *his own son*.

She frowned and her flawless skin went impossibly paler.
'Photograph?'

'*Si*. I pulled files on you back in Courchevel. I saw him
and I didn't even think he could be mine. Didn't even *think*
you would be capable of such a heinous crime.'

His tone was getting louder and louder and he couldn't
seem to stop it.

'I brought you here from the Alps—where you were...
what? Vacationing? Having *fun*, were you, Luciana?' He
felt as if the blood rushed downwards from his head and

there was a roaring in his ears. '*Dios*, no! You were with that sleazy bastard Augustus. Does *he* know about my son?'

'No—no, Thane. He doesn't know. No one does.'

'*Si*. Well, this is fortunate for you both. Still, you didn't even tell me you'd left *my son* behind in Arunthia. I brought you here and you left him there in that…that *place*.'

He was drowning in an ocean of pain. Betrayal.

'I'm sorry but, Thane, I didn't know what to expect from you. You practically abducted me in broad daylight, for heaven's sake!'

What did *that* have to do with anything? Anyway… 'It's a damn good job I did. Otherwise my child would've been lost to me for eternity. Two days you've been here. Not once did you say a word.'

'I…I'm telling you now—'

'Ah, yes. So you are. Did I pass your rigorous testing, Luciana? Am I good enough to be in my son's life now? My son… *My son!* My own flesh and blood and he doesn't even know me.' Something was tearing apart in his chest. 'Well, he will soon enough.'

'You can't go and get him. How will you get past my father? I don't want any fighting or trouble, Thane.'

He jabbed a menacing finger in her direction. 'On *your* head be it.'

With that, he surged across the limestone patio, rubbing his face with his hands.

Within seconds Luciana had gripped his arm, was pulling him round to face her.

'No, Thane. Where my son is concerned you *will* listen to me.'

There was a fierce light in her eyes. As if she had some voracious maternal instinct.

Cynicism curled his lip. This woman? Who'd denied her son his father for more than four years? Thane's father had been a brutally fierce man, but when Thane had asked for him he'd come. Just as Thane should have been given the chance to be there for his son. But, no, he'd had that opportunity *stolen* from him.

'Do you honestly want your introduction to Natanael to be throwing punches or behind prison bars? He isn't like you, Thane. He's not big and tough, resilient and strong. He's small and kind and loving and beautiful, and he's only four years old. Please. Let me go and get him. Bring him here.'

Thane wrenched his arm out of her grasp. 'Let you go and not return? Disappear off the face of the earth? With my son? *Again?* I think not, Luciana. To suggest it just shows how much of a fool you think I am.'

'Then let me ask Lucas to bring him.'

'Lucas Garcia?' he said disgustedly. 'Are you mad?'

'Natanael loves him and Claudia—they're his family. He's with them right now.'

The sharp teeth of anger bit into his heart. '*I* am his family.'

Her eyes closed momentarily. Those long lashes were coated with crystals and it vexed him that he was still noticing such things about her. Vexed him beyond belief.

'Just…please let us make this as easy on Natanael as possible. I don't want him scared. Let him come here on your turf and meet you properly. Peacefully. *Please*, Thane.'

He hauled in air, trying to think through the clattering maelstrom. The last thing he wanted to do was frighten his son; the boy didn't even know him. But he didn't trust Luciana to come back. He didn't trust her at all. Never would again.

Furious that she'd pushed him into a corner, he bit out, 'I will give Lucas Garcia three hours. Then I will go for my son myself and to hell with your father. I will get past him if I have to crush Arunthe Palace into the ground.'

She curled her quivering hand around the base of her throat. 'They'll be here.'

When she glanced up at him, with those brandy tarns full of anguish, for a moment he felt himself falling under her spell. So bewitching. Making him blind to anything but her...

Not any longer.

Thane forced himself to deflect her considerable charms. She'd lured him in for the last time.

'They'd better be here,' he incised. 'I'll never forgive you for this, Luciana. Four years I have missed of him. And if you think I am missing one more day you are grossly mistaken. When he steps foot on Galancia he is here to stay—and so are you. You will not leave here. Neither of you will. We will marry without delay and he will be acknowledged if it is the last thing I do on this earth. And *that* I promise you.'

CHAPTER ELEVEN

LUCIANA STOOD IN front of the double porcelain basin in the sumptuous marble bathroom suite and flipped on the faucet. Cupping her hands beneath the flow, she watched the icy clear liquid pool and then splashed it over her face, dabbing the tender puffy skin beneath her eyes.

Keep it together, Luce. You'll get through this.

She plucked an oyster hand-towel from the rail and patted her face dry, daring to peek at her reflection in the mirror. Lord, she still looked ghastly. And the black jeggings and white shirt she'd chosen to wear didn't help a jot. Not that she cared for her appearance—she just didn't want Lucas to latch on to her wretched state or he wouldn't leave. Didn't want Natanael to pick up on her mood either. This would be hard enough on him as it was.

Insides shaking, she gingerly walked back through to the bedroom…and, darn it, just the sight of those rumpled sheets and the lingering scent of their passion brought the wave of misery rushing back—so tall and wide it flooded over her in a great gush and she couldn't stand up in it. Couldn't even seem to breathe through it.

Crumpling to the bed, she tried her damnedest not to break. Not to splinter apart. She had to stay strong, because the next few days would be hard enough. *Days?* Try weeks. Try a lifetime.

Her conversation with Lucas played back in her mind.

'Please, Lucas, you're the only person I trust to get past

my father and do as I ask. Thane knows. If you don't bring him I don't know what he'll do.'

Already he paced like a caged animal, face dark, implacable. Cold. And if his brutal, austere demeanour wasn't enough for her to know she'd destroyed any chance of happiness between them, his words tormented her heart and soul.

'I will never forgive you for this... We will marry without delay...'

Luciana was unsure what was worse. An emotion-free marriage in which her heart was safe. Or being married to the man who'd always owned her heart and yet hated her in return. And loathe her he did. She'd never forget the look on his face. Such disappointment. Such hatred.

But Nate will have his daddy and you won't have to leave him any time, any place, anywhere. You'll spend every day with him and see him grow into a great man and that will be enough.

Of course it would be enough. It was all she'd ever wanted since the day that little stick had turned blue.

Lucas had promised to be here on the hour—though he wasn't happy about it. His tone had suggested she'd gone stark raving mad. But luckily Claudia had smoothed the way. Thanks heavens for Claudia and her huge heart and quick mind.

Breathe, she told herself. In and out, slow and even as she made her way up four flights of stairs to the vestibule.

The future was staggeringly vague—and wasn't that the story of her life? No idea what tomorrow would bring, how they'd live in this strange place where they didn't know a soul. She was asking herself how they would fit in, how she'd explain to her father that she wasn't taking her crown, how her own people would react on discovering they'd no longer have a new queen in the spring.

Thane had said she'd never leave, but that had to be his anger talking—he couldn't possibly be serious. She'd have to go home before they wed…give a speech renouncing her

birthright. Then enter a marriage she couldn't bear to contemplate. And, *wow*, that seemed to be happening a lot lately.

All of it was churning in a relentless, nauseating roll.
Until she felt insecure. Vulnerable. Defenceless. And by the
time she stepped beneath the overhang of the palatial entryway, restless angst clutched her midsection, making her
bow forward so hard she faked tying the satin bows on her
pumps to cover it up.

*Come on, Luce, you can do this. It's just like being at
home, right? Serene smiles. Cool façade. Think...poise and
grace. By Christmas you'll be a carbon copy of the ice queen
that is your mother and in a barren, loveless marriage.*

Oh, God.

Luciana pinned her spine straight and stood on the top
step, squinting at the black dot swelling beneath the sun.
Plagued by the need for someone to take her hand, tell her
everything would be okay.

No, not someone. Not just anyone.

Chancing a look at Thane, she sneaked a peek towards
the base of the stairs where he stood—separated from her
by metres that felt more like a vast yawning chasm she had
no clue how to fill.

As if he could feel her eyes on him Thane turned his head
to catch her stare. His dark eyes were stormy and full of
condemnation as they snared hers in an unbreakable glare.

She wanted to battle it out with him, make him see her
side of things, but this wasn't the time or place. And deep
down she knew he'd never look at her in any other way. Certainly not the way he had last night. With need and adora-
tion and respect. Something close to joy.

Luciana sank her teeth into her bottom lip, unable to sever
the dark, hypnotic pull, and for a second—when the faint-
est crease lined his brow—she imagined those beautiful
obsidian eyes shimmered with striations of golden warmth.

Hope spun its crazy web inside her...

Then, with a curl of distaste at his mouth, he tore his

gaze from hers. And that web disintegrated into the pit of her stomach.

Deafening, the whoop-whoop of the helicopter grew louder and louder. Her hair whipped around her face and she focused on the only thing that truly mattered.

The colossal machine lowered into a lethal squat on the landing pad in the centre of Thane's huge circular driveway. And the need to run to Natanael—see him, hold him, touch him—had her bolting forward and hurtling down the steps.

At the bottom, Thane snagged her arm to pull her back. 'Wait,' he ordered fiercely.

'Let go of me, Thane.' She felt as if she was hanging by the slenderest of threads over a vast, dark churning abyss and at any moment now the line would snap.

'It is too dangerous—wait a moment.'

He stood with rigid tense-jawed focus, but when the black door swung wide, and Natanael emerged, for a split second he looked as if he'd seen a ghost.

Nathanael careened towards her at a speed of knots. And though he swam in her vision she could still see those gorgeous dimples in his smooth caramel cheeks, those deep expressive eyes so much like his father's.

His father—whose entire body had gone rigid, as though he was desperately fighting to maintain control.

Luciana threw hers to the winds and ran.

Thane had a curious feeling in his chest—as if someone had reached in and taken hold of his heart.

It was like looking at himself. Turning back the clock and gazing in the mirror to see himself as a small boy. And at that moment Thane vowed to do everything in his power to ensure his son would not suffer hurt or cry in pain. He swore it. Swore to move heaven and earth to prevent any of it.

He'd always been adroit at killing his emotions—with the exception of those evoked by Luciana—but he'd never felt anything close to this. Emotions…so many emotions flooding over him. All-powerful. All-consuming.

Natanael—meaning 'God has given'. He tried it out on his tongue for the first time, because maybe he hadn't truly believed it until now, and acknowledged how good it felt—how right.

Thane's fingers burned with the need to touch all that smooth skin, his silky hair—ebony, like Thane's own. But he didn't want to frighten him. The scars on his face were enough to scare anyone, let alone a child.

So instead he ground his feet into the gravel and soaked up every nuance as his son shouted in utter joy, with the biggest smile Thane had ever seen, when he spotted Luciana.

'Mamá!'

Luciana lowered herself into an elegant crouch to catch him and ended up on her bottom in the dirt, not caring about it one iota, hugging him with a glorious smile of her own, smoothing the thick glossy waves of his hair, kissing his brow, his soft cheek.

Never had he seen anything like it. Or maybe he had. Maybe the sight before him resurrected memories he'd rather keep buried six feet under.

Dios, his chest was imploding.

A sweet strum of a giggle flew past Natanael's perfect lips and Thane wondered what she was doing to make him laugh. Saw her fingers tickling his sides, realised he must like that, even though he was yelling, 'Stop! Stop!' And then she was wrapping him in her arms again, kissing him and touching him. All over.

And in that moment there was something so profoundly, exquisitely beautiful about her he felt the strangest sensation in his throat, behind his eyes. Like tiny hot needles pricking.

'Did you see? I was in the big black 'copter, Mamá!'

'I know, darling, and I'm so glad because it brought you to me.'

Darling. The endearment fisted Thane's heart.

'I've missed you so much. My goodness—I swear you've grown an inch.'

Natanael gazed up at her with a fierce male pride that punched Thane in the gut. He was a Guerrero through and through.

When his little mouth geared up for the next zealous outpouring, he stalled—his attention seemingly snagged on Thane.

His insides turned over and he wondered if this was what it felt like to be nervous.

Natanael gaped at him with steady unblinking eyes, scrutinising the scar on his chin as if he couldn't quite believe what he was seeing. Then he looked up at Luciana, and then back to Thane, his tiny mind processing.

It was utterly fascinating, Thane decided. And—for want of a better word—nerve-racking. *Dios*, he felt ill.

Then, as if Natanael had finally accepted Thane was real, he exclaimed, 'Wow! He looks like me. But a whole lot bigger. Do you fly?'

Huh?

'*Si*...actually, I do. I am a pilot and I have my own fighter jet.'

'I knew it,' said Natanael, unequivocally awed. 'You're one of the New Warriors. Did you just come down from InterGalactica?'

Thane blinked. 'Is this in Europe?'

'No, silly. It's in outer space.' With a smile and a nod he gave Thane a knowing look. Then he tried for a wink that scrunched up his entire face as he whispered, conspirator-like, 'You *know* it is.'

Luciana lightly cleared her throat. 'He's into...er...superheroes. Like Batman and Ironman...that kind of thing. And one of them looks uncannily like you. And him too.'

Thane supposed he could live with that. Although what would happen when Natanael asked him to actually fly? He was far too small to go in his military jet.

He hunkered down until they were at eye level and commanded himself to relax, to think of something to say.

'Actually, I *am* a warrior of a kind. I'm the Prince of Galancia and I live here, and I was hoping you would come and live with me too.'

It occurred to him that they'd have to have the 'I'm your daddy' conversation—but, frankly, that petrified him. Plus, he wasn't keen on Garcia being within hearing distance for that. Right now all he wanted was for his son to agree to stay.

Natanael huddled into Luciana, a spark of panic blanching his beautiful face, and Thane realised a second too late his mistake.

'Mamá too?'

He cursed inwardly. Of course he would panic. The love he could feel between them was palpable. 'Yes. Of course. Absolutely. Mamá too.'

Luciana nodded and achieved the perfect smile—though to Thane it verged on brittle, and made him ache even more.

Natanael peered around him, unconvinced. His nose was scrunched, as if he wasn't overly impressed with the tree-lined driveway or the kaleidoscope of manicured blooms flourishing in the borders. Granted, the mansion looked like a one-storey cottage from the top of the cliff. The towering five-floor vista from the beach was far more dramatic and arresting. Though perhaps not for a child.

Thane scratched his jaw. Stumped. Then intuitively he glanced at Luciana. Who, in turn, mouthed a word at him.

He frowned, striving to catch her meaning. What the hell was she saying? 'Dog?' he asked.

'Dog?' Natanael said, perking up. 'You have a dog? *Really*?'

Ah. This, Thane realised, was of great importance. '*Si*. Lots of dogs. And horses too.'

'You have horses?' Dark eyes, the precise shade of Thane's own, grew huge and glittery with excitement.

He didn't seem afraid, so hesitantly Thane reached out

and touched the soft caramel skin of his cheek. The astonishing surge of connection rocked him to the core. Phenomenal. His little boy was the most miraculous thing he'd ever touched. Just like his mother, Thane thought, with a wrenching tug on his guts.

'Many, many horses. You can have your very own. But they don't live here… Yet,' he added hastily, thinking he could easily build a stable for a few. Dozen.

Natanael jumped up and down on the spot. 'I can have my own *horse*, Mamá! Can we go and see the dogs? Right now? Can we? *Can we?*'

Relief poured down Thane's spine. Victory. This was good. He could kiss Luciana for that dog hint. Though he quickly squashed the impulse.

'I think so. Thane, are they downstairs?'

As if she'd experienced the same kind of bone-melting sense of appeasement he just had, she made a clumsy effort at rising to her feet and Thane bolted forward, curled his fingers around her tight waist and lifted her upright.

Surprise widened her eyes. 'Oh. Thank you,' she whispered.

And when he saw her perfect white teeth bite into her bruised red bottom lip a surge of heat spiked his pulse. One he couldn't understand. Didn't want to feel.

Jerking his hands away, he stepped backwards and cleared his throat. 'Pietro will let them out. When I've had a word with Garcia I'll join you.'

With a strained smile she nodded, and glanced at Lucas Garcia herself.

Thane wasn't sure what he'd expected, but it was certainly not her embracing him like some long lost lover. He had to clench his fists to stop from tearing her off him.

'Thank you so much, Lucas,' she said softly, shakily. 'For everything.'

Garcia pulled back and shot her a meaningful look that

pricked Thane's nerves. 'Remember what I said, Luciana. Any time, night or day.'

Another of those frangible smiles, but she brightened it for Natanael and took his small hand in hers—as if she was physically unable to stop touching him. Thane felt an absurd pang of envy that filled him with self-disgust. Surely it wasn't healthy or natural to feel envious of his son? *Dios*, he truly was black inside.

Those clasped hands swayed back and forth as they waltzed into the house, then he turned back to Garcia.

Voice stony, he bit out, 'She will not be contacting you. Everything she needs is right here.'

As if in a standoff, they weighed one another up. One soldier to another.

Garcia's midnight-blue gaze hardened. 'You hurt either of them and I will come for you.'

Thane almost laughed. Almost. Instead he sneered at the other man. 'If you had any sense, Garcia, you'd never set foot on my island again. I've allowed you into restricted airspace to bring my son to me. Next time it will be denied.'

'Do you think that will stop me? I'll be honest, here— I'm not getting a very good vibe between you and Luciana, so I'm not entirely convinced that leaving them here is the right choice.'

'I care very little for what you think. My relationship with Luciana is none of your business.'

'*That* is where you are wrong. She is family, and I will not have her here against her wishes. Are you understanding me?'

Thane's mouth shaped to tell him she was emphatically *not* here against her wishes, but then he realised he'd given her little choice. *Dios*, he'd been so angry. Still was. Couldn't remember half of what he'd said to her.

Whether or not Garcia picked up on his inner turmoil Thane wasn't sure, but he abruptly let loose a sigh that marginally shrank his impressive shoulders.

'Look, I understand this must be a shock—difficult for you.'

Thane wanted to ask him how the hell *he* would know how it felt, but then he remembered the man had just had a child of his own.

'But know this: she has not had one moment of peace in the last five years. Knowing you were out there has tormented her. There is a reason they say ignorance is bliss. She's had to live with her decision for years. Do not forget we have been enemies for a long time, Guerrero. She begged. She bartered. She made a pact. Just to bring Natanael into the world. I know she wanted your son more than anything in this life.'

Begged? Bartered? Meaning Henri had wanted her to destroy their son? For the umpteenth time in history Thane wished he'd pulled that trigger. Vibrated with the urge to rain a hellish firestorm on the man's head. Crush him beneath his almighty foot.

Of one thing he was certain. He would do everything in his vast power to ensure Henri Verbault was erased permanently from his wife's life. And his son's too. Their relationship was officially at an end.

Dios, he was so vexed his insides shook. In fact blistering fury was all he could feel in every molecule of his body as it ran like red-hot lava through his veins. Anger towards every person who'd kept him from his son. He wanted to punish them all.

And that still included Luciana. Because she should have come to him five years ago. He would have protected her from the start.

Thane crossed his lethal arms over his wide chest. 'You love your daughter, don't you? How would you feel if she'd been kept from you for the first four years of her life?'

His voice was iron-hard but he was genuinely interested to hear this answer. What would a normal person feel right now? Should his insides be so black with hatred? Or was he truly twisted with darkness inside?

But then Garcia had to shock him by being brutally frank.

'Not just angry. Furious. Cheated. Betrayed. All of the things you are doubtless feeling. But if I looked at the bigger picture I would see that above all else Luciana put her son—*your* son—first, believing he was unsafe. I have no idea how much of your reputation is true, but one fifth of it would be enough to persuade me. She protected him as any mother would. And I could not hate her or blame her for that.'

On that note, he spun on his heels and strode back to the helicopter.

Thane watched the blades whip into a frenzy, slicing through the air. The vociferous clamour lent him a moment of mental peace. A chance to breathe without it physically hurting.

'I only wanted to keep him safe... We're enemies... I was scared...'

Then the sonorous roar receded and it all came rushing back in one titanic tsunami of agony—and he turned and ploughed his fist into the stone wall.

Dressed in Hawaiian-style shorts and a funky matching T-shirt, Natanael was a red blur, sprinting along the shoreline, dragging a long stick that drew a wavy line in the damp sand, while those great lumbering dogs pranced around him. Her little boy in seventh heaven was a glorious sight to see.

Slanting another glance over her right shoulder, she kept watch for Thane. The helicopter had soared into the sky over an hour ago and she felt flimsy and tenuous—like a kite that would blow away with one gust of wind.

Sloshing through the shallow waters, she slowed her step, 'Hey, Nate? Shall we build a sandcastle and wait for Thane?'

'Sure, Mamá.'

Together they scooped sand into a mound, and Luciana watched those sweet little hands pat-pat-pat their creation into shape. This was good. She had to keep busy. Too much time to think and regret and fret would drive her loopy.

'May I join in?'

She flinched at Thane's low, masculine tone and rocked back on her knees to peek up at him.

'Of course,' she said, her stomach hollowing at the pain that darkened his eyes. At the way he shunted frustrated fingers through the swarthy mess of his hair.

When his hands plunged to his sides her gaze snagged on his raw swollen knuckles and air hit the back of her throat.

'Thane?'

Lord, had he hit Lucas? Reaching up, she dusted over his torn skin.

'Did you fight?' she whispered.

'No.'

He snatched his hand away and she curled her fingers in her lap. He'd closed himself off to her. Emotionally. Physically.

Natanael—oblivious to it all—said, 'Sure, you can help. You can build the moat of the castle if you want. That's a *biiig* job.'

'I think you're right,' Thane said easily, sinking to his knees. 'Where do you think I should put it?'

'Right there.'

Nate pointed to a slope that was close to him, Luciana noticed. As if he wanted Thane closer, in his space.

That was a big enough clue for her and she shuffled backwards, giving them some room, some time together, while her heart lodged itself in her throat. It was like watching a fantasy she'd replayed in her mind, but reality was even more incredibly beautiful.

'Is your name really Thane? Like the warrior?'

Those broad shoulders seized up. 'Yes. But...'

Dark turbulent eyes darted her way in a silent plea that said he didn't want Natanael to call him Thane. Of course he didn't.

'Do you want to tell him now?' she whispered.

Incredible as it was, he blanched—as if drowning in pure fear. Almost as if he expected a rejection.

She couldn't abide it. This was her doing and she didn't want him hurting any more than he already was.

'Nate…' she began. 'You know how Auntie Claudia is Isabelle's *mamá* and Uncle Lucas is his *papá*?'

'Mmm-hmm.'

'Well…' She licked lips salty from the sea breeze. 'Thane is…your daddy. He's your papá.'

His dark head jerked up. *'Really?'*

'Yes.'

A huge smile stretched his face as he looked at Thane, then back to her. 'Oh, *wow*—my daddy is a New Warrior.'

'He is,' Luciana agreed, fighting tears. 'He saved me once. Many years ago.' Her throat felt thick, and it burned as if aflame. Stung so badly her words came out on a choked whisper. 'He's a real superhero.'

She could feel Thane's eyes searing into her cheek, but before either of them could exchange a glance or say a word Nate launched himself at Thane like a cannonball, almost knocking him over.

Luciana watched those big, strong, protective arms curl around their son, wrapping him in instantaneous instinctual love. And knew, no matter what the future held, she'd done the right thing.

So while she kissed goodbye to any chance of a loving marriage those glorious sounds of male bonding were sure to keep her warm at night. And as Nate tugged on Thane's hand, to coerce him down to the water's edge, half of her felt as if she'd lost her little boy. The other half reasoned that there had merely been a part of her son that was never hers to begin with. That part was solely for his daddy.

As for her and Thane… Some things were meant to be. And some things were not.

CHAPTER TWELVE

HIS SON NEVER stopped talking, Thane realised, not even to take a breath. And within three days he had the entire household wrapped around his tiny butterscotch pinkie finger.

He said, 'Christmas tree!' and Pietro was lugging ten-feet-tall firs into the main lounge, trailing dirt across the antique Persian rugs. The biggest monstrosity Thane had clapped eyes on was deftly smothered with garish ornaments and enough twinkling lights to illuminate the Taj Mahal.

To say Thane didn't 'do' Christmas was the understatement of the millennia, since it ordinarily tainted his mind with an abundance of achingly dark memories. But he couldn't seem to say no to Nate any more than anyone else could.

Luciana included.

Which was how now, fresh from his shower and dressed to kill in sharp business attire at the ridiculous hour of seven in the evening, he'd known where to find them. Known she'd be clearing the debris in the kitchen after baking Nate his favourite white chocolate cookies for supper while he happily munched and drank his milky way into bed.

Pandering to his every whim. As if she yearned to be needed. As if she had to keep busy or she'd shatter to smithereens. Not that her outward regal poise had faltered, but he didn't trust that cool façade of hers. It wasn't the real Luciana and it set his teeth on edge. Though he only had himself to blame. By creating this ever-widening gulf between them.

But, *Dios*, he'd felt so volatile after her revelation. Drowning in emotions he was ill-equipped to handle. So angry. Betrayed and devastated. So black inside he'd been petrified to go anywhere near her. Unsure whether he wanted to yell and vent or bury his pain inside her. Beg her to touch him, make him forget—which felt tantamount to an insult to his pride. So conflicted. Torn. His usual ruthless decisiveness obliterated until he felt weak. Less of a man. At the whim of dangerous emotions that no hardened commanding warrior should feel.

Every day he waged an internal war. Knowing that in many ways her arguments held weight. They'd been enemies for centuries. He *had* almost assassinated her father. And for the last three nights he'd been engaged in political warfare with his uncle, who was going to extreme lengths to keep Thane from his throne. Instigating trouble left and right. Leaving Thane uneasy, in no doubt that he needed to get Luciana down the aisle—preferably yesterday. Needed to claim his heir before Christmas. Ensure his absolute safety.

And if this was the way she'd felt years ago—afraid, panicked, verging on desperate to shield their son—Thane would have to be made out of stone not to understand her predicament. His uncle's reputation wasn't founded on fresh air, and nor was Thane's. He was lethal even in his sleep. So, prevaricating aside, could he honestly blame her or hate her for doing what any mother would? *No.*

But all the reasoning in the world wasn't eradicating the ache. Or helping him forget that he'd missed four years of his son. Lost the sound of his cry when he came into the world. Had Nate's first word robbed from his ears. Missed the amazing sight of his first step. And the thought that he couldn't get any of that back drenched his heart in sorrow. Coated his mind with resentment and fury.

It was taking everything he had to switch off, just so he could function like a rational member of society, wrestle for control where he could and pave the way for their future.

Leaning against the kitchen doorframe, he crossed his arms over his chest and did a swift recon of his flour-bombed kitchen. Only to be hit with bone-deep longing, wishing he was a part of the warmth that pervaded the room. But, no matter how much time he spent with Nate, at times like this he felt like an outsider looking in. Unable to breach the dense walls of their love. As if they were the family and he the dark intruder who didn't belong. Unworthy as he was. And envy was so thick and poignant it pervaded his chest, making it hard to breathe.

Then one look at Luciana and he was back to battling in the internal war. Distrusting her. Still wanting her.

Wrapped in a long, thick wheat-coloured cardigan, chocolate-brown leggings and socks that scrunched around her ankles, she looked so young, so adorable. So hatefully sexy. All that lavish honeycomb hair was pinned in a messy knot atop her head, the odd stray tendril curling, caressing her cheek, and when she lifted one hand to brush it away with her wrist she left a smear of creamy buttery sugar streaking her flawless skin.

He wanted to lick it off. Taste the honeyed sweetness of her skin. Let it saturate his tongue.

Damn him to Hades for allowing her to beguile him.

Nate's voice yanked Thane from his turmoil and he watched him swipe at his milk moustache with his Batman pyjama sleeve.

'Eight sleeps until Christmas, Mamá. What would you like from Santa?'

Luciana plopped down into the seat beside him and dabbed his mouth with a tissue. 'I want you to be happy. Are you happy here?'

So loving she was with him. Selfless. Protective. So much like his mother. And Thane realised then that never had he thought so much of his childhood since Luciana had stormed back into his life. Something else to mess with his head, shove him to the edge of sanity.

'Yep. I like living on the beach, and my new dogs, and my new daddy, and my room isn't great...it's *awesome*.'

That would be the room that now resembled outer space, with a galaxy of stars painted across the ceiling that shone in the dark.

'You won't fit into my new spaceship bed tonight, Mamá, so will you sleep with Daddy, like Auntie Claudia with Uncle Lucas?'

Luciana closed her eyes for a beat. 'Er...no, I don't think so, darling. Maybe I'll sleep in the suite next to yours, in case you need me.'

Aversion constricted his throat. Was that how it would be between them? Separate suites? Strangers who shared a house? A son? The thought made him cold to his bones.

'I'm a big boy now,' said Nate, all Guerrero fierce pride. 'You can go further down the hall with Daddy.'

Thane couldn't think of anything worse. Luciana lying beside him in that slippery, silky, lacy black camisole and shorts, that vanilla and jasmine scent taunting his senses. So close yet unable to touch. Bad, *bad* idea. He didn't trust himself not to reach for her when his defences were low. When his anger was asleep. When he craved oblivion from the pain.

Frankly, she didn't deserve to be used in such a way. Since he doubted she still shared their fatal attraction. Since she'd moved in with Nate and shrank from him the odd time he accidentally touched her. As if he were some dangerous predator who would maul her at any moment. And he could hardly blame her for that since it was exactly how he felt. Toxic. Lethal.

Luciana, who was clearly reading from the same map, said vaguely, 'We'll see.'

Nate gave an immense cat-like yawn, hair flopping over his brow, and Luciana stroked the ebony tufts back and smiled indulgently. 'Come on, sleepy-head. Time for bed.'

Heavy eyes blinked up at her. 'Can I have a carry?'

Thane pushed himself off the doorframe. 'I believe that is my job.'

Luciana glanced up and for a split second he was sure he saw pleasure light a fire in her brandy eyes, but then she trailed that gaze down over his attire and the flames flickered and died. He took a scissor-kick in his stomach and when he drew up close suffered another swift jab. She looked like an exhausted Botticelli angel—the violet smudges beneath her eyes a vivid contrast against her unusually pale skin.

And right then he realised they couldn't go on like this much longer. While he'd never wholly trust her again, completely forgive and forget, he had to try and move on—for all their sakes. He just wasn't sure where to start.

Nate found a burst of energy to bounce in his chair and raise his arms. 'Daddy! Will you give me a carry downstairs?'

'I certainly will.'

Down they went, Thane stealing a hug on the way, inhaling that glorious warm bathtime scent, loving those fragile arms wrapped around his shoulders trustingly, giving him a 'squeezy cuddle' right back. He'd been initiated into the realms of squeezy cuddles yesterday, and found they were strangely addictive displays of affection.

Luciana pulled back the star-encrusted navy bedcovers and Thane eased him down and kissed his brow, stroked the back of his finger down that cherubic cheek. 'Sleep well.'

'You too, Daddy.'

He walked to the door as Luciana fussed.

'Love you, tiger,' she said.

Nate mumbled sleepily, 'Love you too, Mamá.'

Thane leaned against the hallway wall outside his room, telling himself to leave now. Avoid confrontation. Any kind of temptation.

His traitorous feet didn't like that idea—suddenly had

a mind of their own, wanted to be with the woman that haunted his body and his mind.

Luciana pulled the door closed and warily met his gaze. *Dios*, she was so beautiful. Made his heart ache. And he couldn't fathom that any more than he could understand anything else he was feeling.

Nate's words from earlier penetrated his brain, and before he knew it he said, 'He expects to see a marriage like your sister's.'

Her eyes drifted downwards to where she scuffed the parquet with the toe of her fluffy sock.

'He does. But all marriages and families are different. He'll learn that too.' Her husky voice teemed with yearning. 'Claudia's marriage is…unique, I suppose. They love each other intensely. Talk constantly. Wouldn't dream of being in separate beds. They married for love, not because of duty or a child. Ours won't be that kind of marriage.'

He knew that, so why a dagger lanced through his heart was a mystery.

'I suppose ours will be more like my parents'. They always had separate beds. It didn't affect me…'

A small furrow lined her brow as she nibbled on the pad of her thumb.

He didn't believe her. Not one iota. Began to wonder if the revered Verbault union was more myth than fact and had affected her in ways he couldn't see. Throw in the longing in her voice and he was more certain than ever that their marriage would be a far cry from what she truly coveted. Which was why he didn't trust her not to run again.

'Where did you sleep last night, Thane?'

Wrapping her arms around her gorgeous curves, she frisked her gaze down his midnight Italian suit, his ice-blue shirt, and he'd swear a shiver rustled over her skin.

'Are you going there again?'

'*Si*. Galancia Castle,' he said easily, unsure why that

would sadden her, or wreak the anxiety he could see clouding her brandy gaze.

He had to grind his jaw to stifle the explanation hovering on his tongue. He didn't want her knowing there was trouble afoot. Didn't want her worrying for their safety. He'd prove to her he could protect them if it was the last thing he did. She hadn't believed in him five years ago, so this time he'd move the planets out of alignment to ensure she did. And if that meant he was running on two hours of sleep, constantly looking over his shoulder in the hellhole that was his birthplace, so be it.

'Guards will be posted here, upstairs and down.'

'All right,' she said, her body deflating as she gazed down the hallway and out of the west-facing double doors, towards Arunthia, in a way that dropped an armoured tank on his chest.

Heart-wrenchingly familiar, it said she wanted to be a million miles away from here. From *him*. It said she wanted to be with her family, with people who truly loved her. Not a black hearted prince. It was a look he remembered well. The look of a woman imprisoned.

Dios, he couldn't bear it. Didn't know how to get rid of it. He'd never been able to with his mother, had he?

He pushed off the wall. Hardened his body into the emotionless indestructible weapon it had been honed to be. Focused on what he could control with some semblance of rationality.

'Nate has asked to see Santa Claus and the Christmas fête is in Hourana this weekend. I was thinking we could all go as a family. For Nate.'

He knew that would sway her so he used it abominably. But they had to go out and paint a united front. Play happy families. Deflect his uncle's attempts at undermining him. Word of his impending marriage had spread like wildfire and his people were in a celebratory mood. It was the perfect time to introduce them.

'For Nate. Right.'

She gave him a short nod and forced one of those serene
smiles that sparked his temper. Made him want to shake it
out of her.

'I'm sure he'd enjoy that.'

Another victory. But no relief in sight. 'Good. I'll see
you in the morning.'

He stepped towards the staircase, stopping when her fingers tentatively touched his sleeve, sending a fresh arrow of
heat through his veins.

'Thane? Please wait. Don't go yet. We need to talk. About
when I can go back to Arunthia.'

Never.

'I need to leave now. Maybe we'll talk tomorrow.'

A soft sigh slipped past her lips. 'I can't marry you without tying up my life at home. I have my own responsibilities. And you said we'd talk about it yesterday, when you
dropped the "we're getting married on Christmas Eve"
bomb on me. As you were walking out of the door, I has-
ten to add.'

That spark of temper ignited in the pit of his stomach and
raged through his body, firing his voice to a blazing pitch.
'*Si*, well, you owe me four years, so I'm damn sure you can
wait another day.'

Guilt thrashed him and he instantly wanted the words
back. He was unsure why he'd said them with such a vicious
lash of his tongue. Maybe because she'd called Arunthia
home. Maybe because he knew she didn't want to marry
him, only wanted to leave, no matter what excuse she gave
herself. Henri was quite capable of tying up her life. She
wanted her freedom. Something he could not, *would* not
give her. His son was here to stay.

Moreover, the date was set, their marriage arranged.
She would become his wife in less than a week. And if the
thought that they had to perform for the crowds tomorrow
wasn't enough to convince him to tame his tongue and start

building bridges, the way she flinched as hurt darkened her beautiful eyes certainly was.

Luciana knew regret when she saw it. Though it still failed to lessen the strike of his words—each one like a knife-blow to her chest.

At the searing impact, his deep pained frown vanished behind her eyelids and the sound of his retreating footsteps gave way to the forlorn thunder of her heart.

Three days of this and she was ready to crack. Living on a knife-edge while a red river screamed through her blood, chanting for her to escape. Sleep was a fool's dream. One day blurred into the next. And stone-cold silences caromed off the oppressive walls until she felt a relentless ache of loneliness that refused to abate.

The only thing keeping her standing—Nate.

Luckily enough she knew the drill. Had seen it all before. And so, with the asset of royal breeding, she kept her head high and smiled on demand. Her mother would be so proud.

Why was he avoiding the subject of her going home? There was no way she could marry him without renouncing her throne. How would *that* look to her people? What was more, she at least wanted her sister at her wedding—but had he asked her who she would like there? No. She'd just been told when and where. Truth was, she couldn't understand the hurry. Why not springtime?

Ah, come off it, Luce, you're petrified. Scared stiff of committing to a loveless marriage. Where you'll be eternally powerless. Trapped by invisible shackles. His mistresses secreted behind closed doors...

Slumping against the wall, she slid to her bottom, bending her knees to hug them to her chest.

Stop. Just stop jumping to conclusions. Stop with the portentous predictions.

Problem was, three days of silence had slowly turned her mind inside out—and with it came unadulterated panic exacerbated by Thane's sporadic vanishing acts. Every day he spent with Natanael, every evening he disappeared until dawn, leaving her with enough bodyguards to secure Fort Knox. His cousin Seve being one of them.

Could the man scream, *I don't trust you not to steal my son* any louder?

She felt like a captive, with no way to escape. And, since he couldn't seem to tolerate the sight of her, was he getting comfort from elsewhere now? Was that where he was? Did she have the right to know who he was sleeping with?

Her mother would say not.

She'd always divined that her mother truly loved her father but it was disastrously one-sided. Luciana could have only been twelve or thirteen when she'd spied one of her father's mistresses slipping down the hall, seen her mother's tear-tracks when Luciana had sneaked in her bedroom to ask about her.

'We don't talk about such things. Go back to bed, Luciana.'

Considering how cold Luciana had felt in the last few days, Marysse Verbault deserved a gold medal for that cool façade she'd perfected. Imprisoned by duty. Funny thing was, Luciana could have put up with all of that from Augustus. But the thought of Thane being in another woman's bed…

Squeezing her eyes shut, she dropped her head to her knees and forced air into her lungs, past the heavy, tumultuous maelstrom that swirled like a thick brume. Tried to cling on to the rapidly fraying threads of hope that he'd come round. That they could somehow find each other again.

She shoved desperate thoughts into her brain to keep faith afloat. Telling herself he'd brought her here for a reason. That she was the only person he could feel. That the fact he wanted them to go out tomorrow as a family meant there was light at the end of the tunnel.

If only she could believe it.   .

CHAPTER THIRTEEN

WHETHER IT HAD been her midnight sniffle-fest to Claudia—who'd told her to stop being such a darn pessimist, painting her future blue when it was only early days, which Luciana conceded was a fair point—or whether it was Nate's hyper-chatty mood as they clambered out of the luxurious bulletproof Range Rover to behold an authentic winter wonderland, she wasn't sure. But for the first time in days her spirits had lifted and she was determined to make the most of their first family affair. To think positive *unpessimistic* thoughts and refrain from pondering on why Thane looked exhausted. What *exactly* he'd been doing all night.

No, she wasn't torturing herself with any of that. Nor was she allowing his invisible power storm to buffet her like a ship in a restless sea. And that ominous slinky dread coiling in the pit of her stomach, warning her that trouble was coming…? Not listening. Not today. Today she was channelling her inner cheeriness—Nate deserved nothing less.

The rich nutmeg and cinnamon scent of gingerbread wafted over her, courtesy of the warm breeze, and she inhaled deeply. 'Wow, that smell is amazing. It's the strangest thing—to be looking at Santa's grotto, surrounded by reindeer and heaps of snow, in twenty degrees—but I've got to admit what they've achieved is fantastic. It's Lapland!'

Slamming car doors, Thane murmured, 'It is…' in that distracted manner he'd worn for days, as if his mind was in constant turmoil.

Guilt and unease weaved in and around her ribcage, and for the thousandth time she wished he would speak to her. Let her past those impermeable steel barricades he'd erected so they could work through this.

'Would you like your bag?' he asked, his voice making a sudden shift to that deep drawl she loved so much, as if he'd just found something amusing. 'You have a tendency to leave them in vehicles and make me fetch them.'

The return of his humour—however slight—was so shocking, so wonderful, she smiled up at him, squinting against the burnt orange and red haze of the lowering sun. 'Yes, please. I would. And, just think…you don't have to send someone to France this time.'

'What a relief,' he said sardonically, even as he frowned. As if he was just as surprised at his quip as she was.

Her heart was buoyed up a little more and she wondered if their moods rubbed off on each other. Vowed to be extra chipper, just in case.

'Oh, actually,' she said, 'I think I'll leave my coat in there. I can't believe how warm it is.'

With a roll of her shoulders she shrugged off her long cream jacket and pushed it into Thane's waiting hand. When that hand didn't move a muscle she glanced up and caught his heated stare—which doused her in his particular brand of fire.

Another return. The first time in days that he'd paid her the slightest attention. And as that searing gaze trailed down her body, from the V-neck of her coffee and cream polka dot dress to her cinched waist, all the way down to the flared kick of the skirt, where the fabric kissed her skin just a peep above her knees, her heart floated higher still and beat an excitable thrum in her throat.

He lingered on her bare calves until she felt positively dizzy.

'You look…stunning, Luciana. Truly beautiful.'

That voice was husky. Intimate. All *Thane*. And wanton

heat surged upwards into her cheeks as her stomach imploded with shameful want.

She dug her cream kitten heels into the asphalt to curb her squirm. 'Thank you. You don't look too bad yourself.'

Understatement. Right there.

Suave and sinfully hot, that commanding body was sheathed in one of his *de rigueur* custom-made Italian suits. The biscuit hue was striking against his olive skin as was the torso-hugging crisp, white open-collared shirt he wore beneath. In short, he oozed gravitas from his every debauched pore, and the brooding expression on his face made him look as dangerous and piratical as ever.

Those dark eyes fixed on her mouth as she slicked her glossy lips with a flick of her tongue. 'Luciana...' he murmured. 'I...'

And when they flicked back up to meet hers a meteor shower of dazzling sensation exploded inside her pelvis.

Oh, Lord, he still wanted her. She knew it. Also knew he was fighting it. Fighting it with all his might. As if his anger lingered and he wanted to hate her but couldn't persuade his body to obey.

'You were going to say...?' she prompted.

His throat undulated on a hard swallow. 'Only that I'd like us to try and be a family today.'

She wanted to ask why. For whose benefit. But caught herself in the nick of time, annoyed at her suspicious mind. Who cared why? He wanted to try and that was okay with her. An enormous step in the right direction.

'I would too,' she said softly. 'And maybe later we could talk?'

The sooner they discussed her going home and their marriage the better for all of them. They couldn't go on like this.

Thane gave her an enigmatic smile that failed miserably to instil her with any kind of confidence. But before she could pin him down Nate burst between them, bouncing on his loafered feet like a coiled spring.

'There's Santa's house! And look over there! A big sleigh! Can we ride in it? *Can we?* Oh... Is that the Three Kings? They look *scary*.' Of course he looked up to his big warrior. 'I don't want to see them, Daddy.'

Luciana watched those wide shoulders relax, watched bad-boy, dominant Thane disintegrate like milk-sodden cereal in the face of all that cherubic idolisation.

'I'll take you to meet them and show you there is nothing to be afraid of—okay?'

Nate didn't look convinced, but climbed up Thane like a monkey all the same. 'Okay. I'm ready.'

'Are *you* ready, Luciana?' Thane asked.

To spend an evening being a family? Something she'd always dreamed of?

'I'm definitely ready.'

Ten minutes. That was all it took to sense that Nate's insuperable case of hero-worship for his father was nothing in comparison to that of Thane's people.

The intense magnetism he exuded grew in strength the further they walked, until he was an imposing impression of vibrant and unrelenting power. But those waves of energy flowed with a palpable warmth that was positively endearing. And for the first time she didn't see a ruthless soldier, born to fight, she saw a prince of the realm born to be King.

It was such a thrilling sight she couldn't calm the flurry of burning butterflies inside her, their tiny gossamer wings stroking her heart with pride and her stomach with want.

The town was utterly delightful. Stone façades with deep wooden lintels and picturesque fairytale windows lined the intricate alleyways, and there was a lovely blend of quaint bespoke shops and chocolate box family homes. A few were a little shabby, and there was a subtle cloud of poverty in the air, but it wasn't so obvious as it had been in the outskirts they'd driven through to get here.

As Thane had told her, his uncle's tyrannical rein choked his people. The fact that they were still so pleasant and joyful was humbling. In truth, she still found it amazing they were so accepting of *her*. The enemy in their midst.

By the time they reached the main square night had fallen, and the colossal fir tree taking centre-stage near the clock tower burst into a dazzling display of a million twinkling stars of light.

Nate gasped in delight, cheering along with the flock of festive gatherers, and Thane laced his warm fingers through hers with a gorgeous half-smile that sent a shower of unadulterated happiness raining over her. It was one of those moments in time she wished she could freeze-frame, because it held the promise of unaccountable tomorrows. Of what might be.

He was trying so hard tonight. And she was determined not to suspect that his efforts were merely for the cameras. The cameras that now flashed around them in a dazzling firework display.

Squeezing his hand, she relished the spark of their fiery magical connection and tugged him towards a carpet of colour: rows of stalls that were a complete festive indulgence. Jingle-bell-shaped cookies. Apples dunked in glossy red candy and Swiss white chocolate. Unique crafts and *objets d'art*. Handmade jewellery and amazing tree decorations— intricate blown glass figurines, hand-carved wooden rocking horses and baubles etched with snowflakes.

Thane bought half of that stall, since Luciana and Nate oohed and ahhed over it all.

The yummy, nutty smell of roast chestnuts and frangipane Stollen floated in the air and lured them to the food tent, where Thane and Nate indulged in pancakes drizzled with chocolate sauce. Luciana chose the Galancian version of mulled wine, its scent heady and seductive, and by the time she cradled her third cup she felt half sloshed.

'Thane, is this stuff strong?'

'A little.' He narrowed those black sapphire eyes on her. 'Do you drink often?'

'Nope.'

'Okay, no more for you.'

His hand a claw on the rim of her cup, he tried to wrangle it from her death grip. Then he pursed his lips to stem the laughter that glittered in his gaze.

'Let go, Luce.'

Luciana peeked up at him through the veil of her lashes, feeling naughty and reckless and so happy that he was smiling again. 'Make me.'

He growled—the sound dangerously feral. 'Are you drunk?'

'Don't be daft. Of course not.'

The tent made her a liar by taking her for a spin.

'Good, because we are going ice skating.'

Oh, heck.

'Fancy a coffee?'

For four minutes Nate was like Bambi on ice—all legs and flailing arms. Not that he was discouraged by smacking off the hard surface every five seconds. Guerreros were made of stronger stuff than that. He just picked himself up, wobbled a little, and off he went again.

As for Luciana, she was all style and grace—but the Galancian mulled wine had put her in a fun-loving, giggly mood that was so infectious it obliterated the darkness that had been festering inside him.

'Daddy, watch *me*.'

Nate perfected a double twirl and Luciana clapped, sending a battalion of bystanders cheering along with her.

Daddy. Why he'd chosen that over Papá was a mystery, but Thane liked it. Every time he heard it his heart did a funny little clench.

Nate suddenly faltered and Thane skated over, scooped him up by the waist and lifted him high into the air like an aeroplane. His huge grin as he squealed in delight etched itself into Thane's memory, his heart.

Time slowed.

Snow drifted lazily from the canopy ceiling as they spun round and round.

Nate screeched his name and whooped with joy. And realisation hit him with the ferocity of a thunderbolt.

He wouldn't even be a daddy at all if it weren't for Luciana, would he? She'd gambled with her reputation, risked bringing disgrace upon her house, her country, overturned the colossal expectations of a royal firstborn heir and fought to have his son out of wedlock. Without her courage Thane wouldn't have this moment. This perfectly wonderful moment in time.

No matter where he'd been for the last four years, no matter what he'd missed, without Luciana he wouldn't be gazing into eyes so like his own. Wouldn't have this precious fragile body to hold, to cuddle or to spin in the air. Wouldn't be able to incite the adorable innocent smile that never failed to lift his soul. Without Luciana he wouldn't have this moment or one hundred more just like it. The opportunity to have a million more after it.

And then came a crack of lightning, incinerating the remnants of his anger, leaving him awash with need. The need to wrap Luciana in his arms and thank her from the bottom of his black heart. Come to think of it, the fact she'd wanted Thane's son so badly at *all* astounded him.

When Nate was safely perched on his blades and had tootled off, Thane instinctively swivelled to find her—and somehow, like a whirl of fate, she crashed into his arms, her gorgeous curvy body plastered flush against his.

'Oops,' she said breathlessly. 'I nearly went over. Are you okay?'

Why? he wanted to ask. *Why did you want my son so badly?* The son of her enemy. That had to mean something. Right?

'Thane?' Affectionate concern etched her brow as she stroked his jaw, rubbed her thumb over his cheek. 'What's wrong? Why are you looking at me like that?'

He speared his fingers into the fall of her hair and dived into her eyes. 'Thank you.'

'For what?' she whispered.

'For fighting for him. Making sure he took his first breath. For telling me now, for trusting me now, so I can have him in my life.'

Tears brimmed in her eyes. 'Oh, Thane, I'm so sorry you've missed so much. If I could turn back the clock I would do it in a heartbeat.'

He believed her. He did.

'I can tell you everything,' she promised in a frantic whisper.

'I'd like that.'

'Every last detail. Show you a million photographs so you can see it all…'

'Shh.' He pressed his index finger to her mouth, then dragged it downwards, curling her plump lower lip, coaxing her to open for him as that ever-present magnetic pull—the one he'd been battling for days, the one he was powerless against—drew them together. And when their lips touched that blistering crackle of electricity jolted through his body, sizzled over his skin, fired heat through his veins. Stronger than ever before.

Luciana made a sound that came perilously close to a whimper and Thane let loose a soft growl as they shared one pent-up breath. Then he slanted his head to find the perfect slick fit, desperate to taste, luxuriating in heady relief, because she still wanted him after he'd put her through hell.

Her hands clutched at his broad shoulders, followed the column of his neck, and slid under his ears into his hair as her tongue skated against his. Thane's danced right back, and the slip and slide of their lips took them higher and higher.

The seductive pull of her mouth was a pure exhilaration he never wanted to end.

Dios, he'd missed her. Missed this.

The rapid flash of cameras lit the air around the vast indoor rink, but it was the joyful chorus of spectators chanting their names that brought him back to earth with a thud.

Ending their kiss, he pulled back a touch and pressed his lips to the corner of her lush mouth, the high curve of her cheekbone, inhaling the rich jasmine and vanilla scent from the decadent tumble of her hair.

'Oh, Lord. We're making out in public,' she said, a smile in her husky voice as she buried her hot face in his neck.

'Want to make out at home instead?' he rasped, curving his hands around her sculpted waist to steady her and pull her tightly against him. *Bad* idea, when the crush of her heavy breasts took his arousal up another notch.

Her wanton sigh of 'Yes…' was a stream of warm air over the skin beneath his ear, coercing a shudder to rip up his spine, and when she lifted her face he grinned at her bright pink cheeks.

If the crowds hadn't adored her before they were soon smitten when she spun to face them and dipped into a beautiful little curtsey, stealing the heart of every Galancian in the room. She was going to be a fabulous queen—he knew it.

As if the crowd had picked up his thoughts they began repeating a mantra: 'Queen Luciana of Galancia!'

Her dark blonde brows nigh on hit her hairline. 'They're a bit premature, aren't they? How bizarre. I'm years away from *that*. And you know what's stranger still? I know you'd gladly take your throne now, but I don't feel anywhere near ready.'

The ice shifted beneath his feet, tilting his world on its axis. 'Of course you are ready—you were born ready.'

'You sound like my father,' she grumbled. 'I may have been raised to be Queen, but I would never have chosen it for myself.'

Dios, he hadn't thought for one minute she would be averse. 'But you were about to take power...'

'Not through choice. I was being pushed early because my father is— Thane?' Her palms splayed down his chest, settled over his pecs. 'Why have you tensed up?'

Rolling his neck to slacken his body, he cursed inwardly at the idea that he was about to give her yet another reason to leave. Not to desire their marriage.

She narrowed her eyes in suspicion. 'Why do I get the feeling I've just stumbled on a landmine that's about to blow up in my face? What's going on, Thane?'

'We'll talk later.'

'Ah, no. You're not fobbing me off this time. I'm missing something here, and you're going to tell me *right now*.'

'Luce, I...' He cleared his throat. 'I will take my crown after we marry next weekend.'

She jerked backwards, her footing skewed, and a sense of *déjà vu* rocked him—the jet back in Courchevel—as he instinctively reached out and snatched at thin air as she dodged him. The loss of her warmth froze the blood in his veins.

Skidding a little, she found her balance. 'Wh...What did you say?'

Something told him he was about to have another battle on his hands. He had to remind himself that he hadn't lost one yet.

'By marrying you, a blue blood heir. I can take my crown four years early.'

CHAPTER FOURTEEN

THE SMILE SHE'D been taught in the cradle carried her through fond farewells and the car-ride back to Thane's beachside mansion to tuck a happy, sleepy Nate into bed, even while her heart was tearing itself apart and her mind was working her into a pained frenzy, connecting the dots.

By the time she walked into the suite that had been her palatial prison for days the riotous flow of turbulent emotions was a swirling, churning, flaming volcano at critical mass. And she fanned the flames of that anger—because the alternative was crumbling, breaking, shattering and she steadfastly refused to be that woman. The very woman she'd found curled up against the wall last night in the hallway. Loneliness burrowing into her stomach. Fighting defeat. Almost broken. Allowing *him* to control her. All for what? Because she was desperate for the love of the dark Prince?

Clearly it wasn't him who was crazy. It was her. She should know better. Since when had love or romantic happiness ever entered the equation of her life? *Never.* From the day she'd been born she'd been a means to a crown.

Her hands shook as she gripped the bed-rail and lifted one foot like a flamingo to tug off one kitten heel, then switched legs to yank off the other. And when she spied Thane walking through her door, his dangerous stride a purposeful prowl, only to close it behind him and lean against it, crossing his arms over his shirt-clad chest, ready for battle, she *blew*.

She launched her shoe across the room to clatter off the

wall—and, *God*, that felt great!—then spun on him like a
furious firestorm.

'You seduced me for your crown, didn't you? You played
me from the start—abducted me from Courchevel, brought
me here against my wishes—to get you your throne. *Didn't
you*?'

'You could say that,' he hedged, his easy stance bely-
ing the tension emanating from his honed, dominant frame.

How she didn't go over there and slap his hideously handsome face, she'd never know.

'Makes perfect sense, really. Why else would you want
me "very, *very* badly"?' she bit out, throwing his perfect
passionate prose back in his face. 'Your scruples really are
abhorrent—do you know that?'

Fool, she was. Total, utter fool. She'd known he had an
agenda but, as always, self-preservation had taken a darn
hike and cowered in the woods with this man.

There she'd been, protecting Nate from a power-play,
and she'd walked headlong into the lion's den. Blind to the
warning signs flashing in glaring pink neon, brighter than
a Vegas strip. Hanna and Pietro going on as if she was their
saviour, for starters…

He'd played her like a puppet on a string. And she'd followed his every beat.

She didn't miss the way he shifted slightly on his feet,
thrust his despicable hands through his hateful hair.

'Luciana…angel…'

'Ah, no, Romeo. You can forget the charm. No longer re-
quired. You've got me right where you wanted me. *Bravo*,
Thane. Really, you should be proud.'

Was that her voice? That fractured aria of sarcasm and
bitterness—that portrayal of a heart betrayed?

He rubbed at his temple as if she was one of those Su-
doku puzzles that twisted her brain into knots.

'I cannot see the problem, Luciana. You didn't wish to
marry Augustus and so we would both benefit.'

Of *course* he couldn't see the problem. While he'd been polishing his crown she'd secretly been building castles in the sky. But that was *her* problem. Not his. One she'd simply have to accept. Because she'd given him the one guarantee that would get her down the aisle: Natanael. Not that she'd ever feel regret over that. Seeing them together made remorse utterly impossible.

Now all she had to do was face those portentous predictions she'd been battling for days. A loveless prison of an autocratic marriage would be her future if she wasn't careful.

With a shrug she tore off her coat and slung it to the bed. 'See, Thane? Right there. *You* decided we would both benefit. *You* made that choice for me. Much like the wedding you arranged yesterday, behind my back. Has it never occurred to you that I would like to be asked?'

Hopeless, pathetic romantic, she was.

'I told you the other day we were getting married.'

'Precisely. You *told* me.' But she hadn't argued the toss, had she? No,' she'd allowed him to control her. For the last time.

He hiked one devilish brow. 'So what is the problem?'

She shot him a glare which he impudently ignored.

Lord, he just didn't get it, did he? While she could feel the ropes of a noose tightening around her neck.

From the start it had been the same. No choices. No requests. Only kidnappings and kisses and demands. Either it was ingrained in him to dominate, literally stamped into his DNA, or he respected her so little he didn't value her opinion or her own wishes. Whichever the case might be, what kind of marriage would they have? A hell of a lot worse than her parents'—she knew that much.

Her lungs drew up tight, crowding her chest until she could barely breathe. She'd been under the command of a control freak all her life and suddenly she couldn't commit to a moment longer. Heaven help her, she would *not* live under another man's rule for eternity.

'The problem is,' she said, pleading with her strength not to fail her now, 'I would like some control over my life. To at least be involved in decisions. I would like a partnership, Thane. *Not* a dictatorship. You talk about giving your people a voice. Yet you silence mine. Don't you think that's hypocritical?'

'That is absurd, Luciana,' he said fiercely. 'You speak when you wish to and I listen.'

She groaned aloud. The man was delusional.

'Did you listen in Courchevel, when I told you I wasn't getting onto that plane? *No.* Did you listen when I told you I had to go home before we could get married? *No.*'

A frigid draught swept over her, pebbling her skin with goosebumps.

'*Home*?' he incised. 'Galancia is your home.'

It wasn't his words that bothered her—it was his granite-like tone. The one that said Arunthia was to be forgotten and she should accept that.

He'd have to bury her six feet under first.

She wrenched open the antique armoire and hauled out her suitcase.

'Luciana? What the hell are you doing?'

'What does it look like I'm doing, Thane?'

She was leaving this place. This island. As soon as the dawn broke. And *nothing* would stop her.

'I don't think—'

'Oh, Thane, right now I don't care what you think. And if I were you I would start listening to me. Because your days of controlling my life are *over.*'

Frustration mounting, his pulse spiked, making him feel light-headed as Luciana whirled around the room like a tornado, shoving clothes into the sinister suitcase that sprawled over her bed like a black stain on pure white satin.

'Would you like to tell me why you are packing?'

He had no idea why—she wasn't going anywhere.

Seeing her beautiful clothes and those delicate bottles of cream that made her radiant skin smell sweet being haphazardly tossed into that vile contraption made his fists clench into thwarted balls of menace.

'I would've thought that was obvious. I'm leaving. I need to go home for a few days. I need time. I need to sort out my responsibilities there. If you had stood still long enough this week we would've already had this discussion—but, no, you dictate and you command. And I've *had* it.'

Darkness fell over his eyes until he was blind to everything around him. She was not leaving him again. Nor was she stealing his son a second time.

'No, I am sorry, Luciana, but you are not going anywhere. And *that* is final.'

His conscience was screaming at him to stop. To think about what he was doing. Saying. But if he let her go she wouldn't come back. He knew it. Just as she hadn't five years ago.

Her heavy sigh infected the air. 'You need to trust me, Thane.'

'*Trust*?' The vicious swirling cyclone in his chest picked up pace and he whirled on her in a gust of fury. 'Trust the woman who disappeared in the night and never told me I had a son? Are you *serious*, Luciana?'

Those thick decadent eyelashes descended and her voice turned heartbreakingly weary. 'I know it's early days, but are you *never* going to forgive me? Are we ever going to get past this?'

The memory of earlier tonight, when he'd peered through a different lens...her frantic whisper that she would show him what he'd missed...doused the furious fire in his blood.

He thrust his fingers through his hair and exhaled heavily. 'I'm trying, here, Luce.'

Truth was, even before this evening he'd started to appreciate the turbulence she must have gone through. Which was why he didn't want her or Nate anywhere near Henri

Verbault—the man who'd almost cost him his son. Thane would never forgive him or trust him, and he was amazed Luciana could contemplate either. Obviously she was blind to the man's influence over her, so Thane would protect her from that too. By keeping her here with him.

'Just let your father deal with the Arunthian crown. He places it above your importance anyway. You don't need to go back and see your family ever again. You have Nate and I.'

Her hand plunged from where she'd pinched the bridge of her nose and her jaw dropped agape as she spluttered, 'Of *course* I need to see them. You can't expect me to give up my family. That's just *insane*… Whoa—hold on a minute. Did you expect me to get married next Saturday without my family there?'

'Basically? Yes. I do not want your father anywhere near my wedding.'

'And what about my sisters? My *sisters*, Thane! And, no matter what grudges you have against my King, he's still my father and he's sick. I don't know how long he has left and—'

That stopped him in his tracks. 'He is sick? I didn't know this.'

She flung her arms wide in an exasperated flourish. 'Why *would* you? Since you've never asked or cared to know about that part of my life. If you had you'd know why I was being pushed into taking *my* crown early.' Her smooth brow pleated and she shook her head. 'It's almost as if you haven't accepted who I really am. Do you still wish I was the nobody you met in Zurich, Thane? Have you even acknowledged that I'm a Verbault?'

He flinched. Actually flinched. And he wasn't sure who was more surprised.

'Oh, my God.' A humourless laugh burst from her mouth. 'Did you honestly believe giving me your name would erase my heritage? Stop me from being my father's daughter?

Even if I become Queen of Galancia I will still be a Verbault in *here*.'

With her fist she thumped her chest, and when her voice fractured he felt the fissure in his own heart.

'I'll still be the enemy. You are kidding yourself to think otherwise.'

Pivoting, she spun back to the dark wood armoire, yanked open another drawer and scooped up a mound of pretty, frilly, lacy garments to dump in her case.

Thane slumped against the wall, rubbing over his jaw, his mind going a mile a minute.

In a way she was right. He'd never truly acknowledged who she was: a sister, a daughter, a friend, even the heir to the Arunthian throne. Simply hadn't wanted to admit it to himself. Not because she was his enemy, but because he would have been slammed up against the naked truth—she had responsibilities of her own. To her family, her people. Responsibilities that could take her away from *him*.

So not once had he considered or asked if she wished to take her rightful place. Because he feared her answer. Was scared she'd choose her crown over his. Her family over him.

Self-loathing crawled through his veins. He was so selfish with her. Was it any wonder desperate panic loitered in her brandy-gold eyes—a silent scream that confessed she wanted to be away from here? From him. It cut his black twisted heart in two.

And the way she eluded his own gaze struck him. The night his mother had died Juana Guerrero hadn't been able to look at him either. Her every move premeditated, she'd known what she'd devised. Just as Luciana did. She'd move heaven and earth to leave him. Permanently.

Luciana was kidding herself if she believed otherwise. Why else pack her every solitary possession into that case? A case he hadn't failed to notice had been already half full of Nate's clothes when she'd opened it.

The walls began to loom from all sides and suddenly ev-

erything appeared malefic and pernicious. Even the black
rails of the ironwork bedframe seemed to uncoil and distort
and writhe in front of him. Every drawer she flung open
clattered and squealed and rattled, as if it bore the menacing teeth of a monster.

'You are wasting your time, Luciana. There is no way
for you to leave here.'

'I'll ring Lucas to come for me.'

His heartbeat raced, threatened to explode. 'I will deny
him access to Galancian airspace.'

She froze in her frenetic rush, head jerking upright, eyes
slamming into his. Even from the other side of the bed he
could see her glorious, voluptuous frame vibrate with pique
and pain.

'Are you serious?'

'Deadly.'

Up came her trembling hand, her fingers curling around
the base of her throat. 'You can't do this, Thane. I am *not*
your property. I am my own person. And you can't keep me
here against my wishes. It isn't right. I've felt like a prisoner
in this house for days.'

Her pitch escalated as her breathing turned choppy, raspy,
and she clutched her chest as if struggling for air.

Every ounce of his blood drained to his toes and a cold
sweat chased it. Bolting forward, he thrust out a pleading
hand. 'Luciana, calm down.'

'No, you need to *hear* me this time. What I said before—
it's right and you don't see it. You don't listen to me.' Her
eyes pooled with moisture, making them overly bright. 'By
controlling me you take away my choice. You silence my
voice. My whole life I've had this gag around my mouth,
and I can't *breathe* when I think I'll have a lifetime of that
with you.'

Thane raked his hand around the back of his neck, tearing at the clammy skin. He did *not* silence her; he only
wanted what was best for her. She hadn't wanted to marry

Augustus. He only wanted them here so he could keep them safe. Protect what was his. And yet his conscience argued vehemently. Because he *had* told her she was marrying him. And he knew precisely why—even if he wasn't eager to admit it.

She collapsed against the hardwood drawers as if she no longer had the energy to stand upright. 'For once, just *once*, I would love someone to ask me what I truly want. Everyone who is free in the world is asked that very question every day, I imagine, and I often wonder if they realise how precious it is. If they take it for granted. I want to yell and scream at them that they shouldn't. They should cherish it. I *envy* them, Thane. I envy their freedom of choice.'

It was like being tossed into the past, hearing his mother's wistful voice—the hopes of a woman trapped like a bird in a gilded cage. And suddenly he felt like the damnable hypocrite Luciana had claimed him to be. He refused to ignore the truth one second longer. The reason he had never given her a choice.

'What are you saying, Luce? You don't want to marry me?'

'No, Thane,' she said, shaking her head, her brow pinched. 'I don't.'

And when one single diamond teardrop slipped down her exquisite face he felt as if noxious venom infected his veins, surged through his body, making him destructive, malevolent, black. As if he contaminated her with his darkness.

What more proof did he need than the evil voice whispering in his mind to *make* her marry him? Force her by threats to take away her son. And that disgusted him. It made him sick to his stomach even to think of it. The idea he was turning into his father.

She smoothed her hand over her midriff, as if he made her ache inside, but her tone strengthened as if she was resolved. Her stance one of weary resignation. 'But I will marry you. For my son. He needs you and he loves you.'

Thane closed his eyes. Why didn't that make him happy? Why couldn't he be satisfied with that?

Verity hailed down on him in an icy blizzard, pummelling his flesh through to his bones. He longed for her to want only him. For Thane to be enough.

Idiot, he was. He'd done the one thing he'd sworn he'd never do. He'd let her creep past his defences. *Again*. And that petrified him—because he'd never be enough to make her happy. Just as he hadn't been enough for his mother. To make her want to stay. He was too much like the man he'd sworn he'd never be. Twisted, selfish, possessive, dark inside.

Look at her, his inner voice whispered.

She was so beautiful she made his breath catch, his heart stall in his chest. But that solitary tear-track that shimmied a pearlescent dew down her cheek said it all. It said that one day she would hate him for imprisoning her here. Despise him. It said that one day she might fly to her death with a euphoric look of peace on her face as she finally found freedom. From him. From her life here.

And he couldn't do that to his son. Take away the woman who loved him beyond Thane's wildest imagination.

He wanted Nate to be happy. Have the kind of childhood Thane had never had. Peaceful and joyous. Learn how to be a good man with a pure soul and to be able to love another with his whole heart. Surely that was the greatest gift he could give him? More than horses and dogs and spaceships and candy canes. And to be that person Nate needed Luciana. Not Thane.

Unchaining the doors to the cage, he threw them wide open, his throat so swollen and raw every syllable hurt. 'You are right, Luciana. Of course you are right. You need to go back.'

That glorious body slumped as she gave him a tight, grateful smile. 'We'll just be gone a couple of days. Back for this...this wedding on Christmas Eve—'

'No.' He cut her off with a shake of his head, commanding his tone not to falter, to stay strong. 'There is no need. No hurry. Spend Christmas with your family if you like.'

That had been his mother's worst time for missing her loved ones. Had once made blood trickle from her wrists as the depths of her depression found no bounds.

Unwanted, harrowing, his dark, tormented mind made one of those incongruous leaps, placing Luciana in that bloodbath...

Dios, maybe her leaving long-term was for the best after all. It would only be a matter of time before he destroyed her. He'd rather have her alive somewhere else in the world than dead by his side. And, while he truly believed Luciana had more strength than his mother had, Thane could easily kill her spirit—was already doing so—and that would be a great tragedy in itself.

He lavished himself with one last long look. At that incredible dark bronze tousled tumble of hair. The perfect feminine curves of her body. Those big, beautiful brandy-gold eyes now swimming in confusion.

'Well...if you're sure,' she said, relief blending seamlessly with her bewilderment. 'We could think about getting married in the New Year. But don't you want to spend Christmas with Nate? He'll miss you.'

'No,' he said, turning his back on her, unable to lie to her face as he strode to the door.

If he thought for one second that she might come back he would hold out hope. And it had almost killed him waiting night after night in Zurich, praying she'd walk through the door. A second serving of that persecution would ruin him.

Fingers curled around the door handle, he pushed his final retort past his lips. 'I won't force you into a marriage you don't want, Luciana. In the long run that will only harm Nate. I'll explain to everyone that things haven't worked out between us.'

'Wha...What do you mean? What about Nate? Your crown?'

'I'll find another way.'

There *was* no other way. But in that moment he realised he'd crawl through the dust of his heart to give her what she wanted, needed. He'd make up for the delay to his people somehow.

'As for Nate—we will arrange visits.' Though how he'd manage to say goodbye every time, he wasn't sure.

'Thane? Turn around—look at me, please.'

He couldn't. He'd change his mind.

'I'll arrange a jet for early morning. But I can't be here when you leave. I'll be at the castle. Business.'

The barracks was his destination, and he knew it. He needed to be out cold when she left. He didn't trust himself otherwise. And there was no better way to vanquish his emotions than via his father's legacy.

'Be careful, Luciana. Love my son for me.'

'Thane, *please* wait. Talk to me.'

The soft pad of her footsteps sounded behind him and he momentarily stalled as her sensual jasmine and vanilla scent curled around him in an evocative embrace, luring him back.

No. No more talking. He didn't want her to see what lay beneath. Something too dark to describe.

Thane hauled open the door before she could touch him and vaulted up the staircase to the foyer, where he snatched his keys from the side table and stormed into the night.

CHAPTER FIFTEEN

TWELVE HOURS LATER thousands of miles separated them, and not only was Luciana still reeling from their final showdown but the man refused to leave her be.

Blind to the lush Arunthian vista as the car snaked up the steep incline towards the palace, she saw only those intense obsidian eyes searching her face before he'd sped from her suite, as if he were committing her to memory, as if she were the brightest star in his universe—it was a devastating impression she couldn't erase.

Nor could she erase the questions trying to wade through her woollen, sleep-deprived brain—why was he suddenly willing to give up twenty-four-seven access to his son, delay taking his throne?

Because despite his inglorious method of coercing you into Galancia, his intentions were pure. His only thought was for his people, and he wouldn't force you down the aisle for anything.

And she couldn't have made her desires clearer, could she? *No.*

A fiery arrow of self-censure tore through her chest and she squeezed her eyes shut. *'No, Thane, I don't want to marry you.'* But in that moment—that gasping, suffocating moment—she truly hadn't. Had only envisaged a life of dictatorship, one-sided love and the misery of duty. Where she became a dark blonde replica of her mother.

And that had petrified her. Thrown her into a panic that

had whirled out of control. Muscles burning, aching to run and never, *ever* return. And the idea that she could consider, even for a millisecond, parting him from Nate again made shame crawl over every inch of her skin.

With a restless shake of her head she cuddled Nate to her side, forcing herself back to the present, and glanced up at the fairytale façade of Arunthe Palace—all cream stone walls and fanciful turrets with conical slate roofs— as the car rocked to a stop outside the grandiose scrolled iron gates.

And when the habitual dread *didn't* pervade her body, *didn't* line her soles with lead, suddenly, astoundingly, she watched a smile play at her mouth in the reflection of the window. Apparently battling with the dark Prince had given her the courage to face anything. Even her mother's disapproving glare and her father's steely, vexed countenance as he rehashed her latest escapades in reckless rebellion.

But, unlike five years ago, he would not make her feel guilty, dirty, shameful or unworthy—he no longer held that power over her. She *refused* to grant it to him. It was not wrong to want her son or to wish for the hedonistic passions of love. To reach beyond her expectations. Thane might fight dirty at times, but at least he fought. *Hard.* For what he believed in, what he desired above all else. Taking a leaf out of his book wouldn't hurt.

Thinking about it, right at this moment she'd never felt so strong in her life.

Claudia—tall and dark, striking and radiant—appeared at the arched entryway, shielding her eyes from the sun, and leather creaked as Nate bounced at the sight of her.

'Go inside with Auntie Claudia, darling. I'll just be a few minutes.'

'Okay, Mamá,' he said, darting from the car and bolting up the stone steps.

Luciana raised splayed fingers—*five minutes?*—and on her sister's nod, the door slammed shut.

The locks clicked into place and she depressed the internal speaker for the driver.

'Another limousine, another town. How are you, Seve?' She'd swear she'd seen more of this man in the last few days than Thane.

Down came the privacy screen on a soft whirr, until she stared into deep-set titanium eyes sparkling with amusement in the rearview mirror.

'You beat me to it. I'm impressed. What gave me away?'

'Let's just say I can feel his protection.'

All around her. Wrapping her in warmth when she was so cold inside, missing him already. Wondering what he was doing in that darkly disturbing castle, who he was with. Why her inner voice shrilled that he was with no one, had only his dark pain for company.

'How does it feel, driving a car embellished with the Arunthian royal crest?'

Seve grimaced, and she couldn't help but laugh a little.

'So...are you my new shadow?' she asked.

'I sure am. Until he's satisfied you're safe and that your father won't push you into anything you don't want.'

Wry was the smile that curved her lips. Leopards and their infallible spots. He couldn't quite let go. And the hell of it was she adored him for it. They might not share love, but he cared.

'What is he doing in that castle, Seve? Who is he with?'

Unease permeated the air-con cooled air and he rolled his brick-like shoulders.

'Please, Seve, he won't talk to me.'

Exhaling heavily, he met her gaze in the rearview mirror. 'If I know Thane he's into his third bottle of Scotch after a bout in the barracks while my dear old dad cracks open the champers, celebrating his continued reign.' Anger rode his tone hard. 'I don't know what infuriates me more.'

Luciana frowned deeply. 'Barracks? What would he be doing there? And, hold on a sec—your dear old dad?'

He arched one dark brow. 'Much like Thane, I lucked out in the father stakes. My dad is Franco Guerrero.'

'Oh, Lord.' It struck her then, with everything that had gone on last night, that she'd never given Thane's uncle a thought. 'By marrying me Thane would have overthrown him. I imagine he isn't best pleased about that.'

'Understatement of the millennia, Princess. He's been causing Thane trouble for days—ever since you dropped the Nate bomb on him.'

She groaned aloud. 'Dammit. *That's* why he's been going to the castle. Practically pushing me down the aisle. Why didn't he tell me? The insufferable man doesn't *talk*.'

But she knew the answer before Seve muttered it. He wouldn't have wanted her worrying. Had to be the hero, didn't he? While she was doing her usual—painting a prophesy of desolation in a gilded cage.

Why did she *do* that? Claudia was right—she was a darn pessimist. An optimist would believe fate had brought them together again, regardless of Thane's agenda, say they had a son and that in time love could grow. An idealist would reason that duty didn't necessarily bode a farewell to happiness. They were not her parents—they could strive to have both.

And the duty that put the fear of God up her didn't have to be a noose around her neck—it could be an adventure with Thane. The greatest adventure of all. She just had to fight for it. Make it happen. Be her own hero. And maybe Thane's too, for once. Give him the crown he so desperately wanted. Help him free his people from tyranny. Make his mother's dreams come true. The woman he couldn't even speak of without pain engulfing him with a tenebrous shroud.

'His mother…' she began warily. 'Does he ever talk about her?'

'Never. The world could end tomorrow and he'd die with those memories locked in his soul. She was a manic depressive, you know? She self-harmed and…' Seve blew out an anxiety-laden breath. 'That's why I hate him being in that mausoleum. Makes him blacker than night.'

Panic gripped her stomach at the thought of him hurting somewhere she couldn't reach. 'Listen, I need a couple of days here. So right now you're going to go back there, tell him I'm fine—perfectly safe—and get him out of that castle for me. Aren't you, Seve? Tell me. Give me the words.'

He gave her an incredulous look that said *hell, yeah*, which did a somewhat splendid job of easing the crush in her lungs.

'Good. Okay. And after that I need a favour. Or three…'

A few days later. Christmas Eve.

He had the hangover from hell. Why Seve had ordered him to haul his 'sorry ass' out of bed and get in the shower he'd never know. That Thane had actually obeyed the man was even more incongruous. All he'd wanted was to sleep through Christmas. After that he knew he'd be fine. Great. Wonderful.

His groan ricocheted off the onyx marble as he braced his hands, palms flat, against the shower wall and dipped his head beneath the deluge. The cold water was like shards of glass, biting into his scalp and skin. And this was *post* eight shots of espresso. Some big tough warrior he was. He was just glad Nate wasn't here to see his hero slide down the drain, and Luciana—

Ah, great. He'd just blown his 'I won't think of them for ten minutes' pact.

The floor did a funny tilt—his cue to jump ship—and he stepped onto the rug, wrapping a towel around his waist.

Spying a bottle of headache relief on the countertop, he

reached for it, his hand freezing in mid-air as a shard of light sliced through the dim haze.

'Turn the damn light off, Seve!' he hollered. Was he trying to split his head open?

'Not Seve,' said a delectable honey-drenched tone. 'And, no, I don't think I will.'

His heart stopped. His jaw dropped. And he stared at the door that was cracked ajar. Was he hearing her voice now? His mental state was seriously disturbing these days.

With a shake of his head that made him curse blue when his brains rattled, he turned back to the basin and picked up his razor.

'Are you going to be in there all day? I'm gathering dust, aging by the second, out here.'

Clatter went the blade into the porcelain sink.

He watched his hand move at a snail's pace towards the handle…fingers curling, gripping. Heart leaping, hoping, as he eased the door fully open.

Two steps forward and—*Dios*…

'Luciana?'

Hallucinating or not?

Perched on the vanilla-hued velvet chaise longue, one leg crossed over the other, she rested her elbow on her bent knee and propped her chin on her fist. But it wasn't the sight of that exquisite serene face that jolted his heart back to life, it was the seraphic vision she made dressed from head to foot in ivory-white.

The gown was pure Luciana. No fuss or bustles or froth. Simply elegance that sang a symphony of class. Straight, yet layered and sheer, with a sensual V neck and a pearl-encrusted band tucked beneath her breasts. Lace was an overlay that capped the graceful slope of her shoulders and scalloped around her upper arms in a short sleeve. And atop her head was a diamond halo from which a gossamer veil flowed and pooled all around her.

He rubbed his bare left pec with the ball of his hand

where he ached—God, did she make him ache—and those hot needles pricked the backs of his eyes.

'Luciana…' Her name was an incoherent prayer, falling from his lips. 'You look so beautiful. Like an angel.'

She gave him a rueful smile and spoke softly, 'I've told you before, Thane, I'm no angel.'

Whether it was because he felt utterly broken inside, or because the sight of her had turned the gloomy morning into pure sunshine he couldn't be sure, but his mouth opened and for the first time in his life he was powerless to stop what poured free.

'But you were *my* angel. And you never stopped being mine—not for one minute. Even when I was furious with you, you were still my only light in the dark. And no matter where you are in the world that will never change.'

Down came long lashes to fan over her flawless cheeks as she bit down on her lips. Lips she now covered with trembling fingers.

Panic punched him in the gut. 'Luce?' He took a tentative step closer, relieved when she breathed deeply, pulling herself up to sit tall and straight, with a gorgeous watery smile just for him.

'My sister,' she said, with an airy wave that belied that quivering hand, 'who is somewhere around here, tells me it's bad luck to see the groom before the wedding—but you know what I think?'

While Thane knew nothing about these things, the fact that she resembled a bride and spoke of weddings and grooms wasn't lost on him—but hope was a fragile beast he tethered. Because despite the agony of losing her he would not take her down the aisle without happiness in her heart.

Brushing his wet hair back from his face, he eased down onto the edge of the bed, never taking his eyes off her in case she disappeared. 'What do you think, Luce?'

'I think we make our own luck. I think fate offers us opportunity but *we* are the masters of our own destiny. I think

I've allowed people to control me for too long, and now I'm going to take my life and my happiness into my own hands. Are you ready, Thane?'

Happiness.

He was ready for anything as long as she didn't leave.

CHAPTER SIXTEEN

SHE WAS GOING to propose. Any minute now.

It wasn't every little girl's dream. But, when you'd been governed since the day you were born, being the commander of tomorrow was a unique dream all its own.

So here she was. Sitting opposite a handsome man—*the* most beautiful she'd ever seen. The dark, dangerous divinity that was Prince Thane of Galancia. And maybe she hadn't set the stage so superbly—no dimly lit chandeliers or intimate tables for two, but it was *their* scene, their intimate paradise—the place where she'd been reunited with the other half of her soul—and to her it was perfection. Beyond price.

So all that was left were the words.

And Princess Luciana Valentia Thyssen Verbault had to press her palm to her stomach, desperately trying to calm the swoop and swirl of anxious butterflies, their dance wild with exhilaration and anticipation, before she stood tall. Because she had the horrible feeling she might pass out. She'd felt less nervous renouncing her throne yesterday, before hordes of press. The news would be broadcast at twelve noon and by then—hopefully—she'd be this man's wife.

Sucking in a shaky breath, she rose to her feet and walked over to where he perched on the edge of the bed, his honed body glistening, those black sapphire eyes holding hers captive. And, despite the fact he looked like hell, the mere sight of him, in all his myriad beauties and unguarded mercies, still made her weak at the knees.

Down she went onto the floor before him. Never leaving his gaze, loving the way he opened his legs to let her in. The way he reached up hesitantly, fingers trembling, as he brushed a wayward curl from her temple.

'Luciana…' he murmured. 'I…' A faint crease lined his brow. 'What are you doing down there?'

'I'm doing this right. On one knee.'

'Doing what right?'

When light dawned, he shook his head vehemently.

'Like hell you are.'

He grasped her waist and lifted her up, plonking her astride his knee with a rustle of her skirts.

'You will not kneel before me. And isn't that *my* job?'

'Not when we're living in this splendid era called the twenty-first century, Thane.'

Not when she heard that hint of panic in his voice—the one that reminded her of the day on the beach with Nate. That fear of rejection. She could kick herself for not considering it before. That by taking away her choice he gave her no option to say no. To reject him. Lord, it was amazing what a mess two people could make in a few days.

Wriggling back, she tried to clamber off his lap. Thanks to Thane, she somehow ended up on the bed, where she hoisted up her skirts—slipping and sliding as tulle and chiffon met satin sheets. By the time she was on her knees again she felt like a triathlete after a three-day event. Likely resembled one too, with her tiara askew. But one look at the man of her dreams, wearing a towel that left *nothing* to the imagination, getting on his knees too, as if he needed them equal, and her every thought zeroed in on him. Only him.

'And why shouldn't I kneel before you?' she said. 'I respect you. I'm proud of you. For breaking free of your father's hold, for fighting for your people.'

She trailed her fingertips down the scimitar line of his jaw and stared into those beautiful dark fathomless eyes.

'You're going to be a powerful and noble King and I'll

be honoured to stand by your side. Our son needs a won-derful daddy too, and that man can only ever be you. And *I* need the man I love with my whole heart to be with me always. So…Thane Guerrero of Galancia…will you do me the great honour of becoming my husband?'

His throat was convulsing, and his magnificent chest shook as if he fought his emotions. Until one rogue teardrop finally spilled on his first spoken word.

'L…Love? You *love* me, Luciana?'

Holding his jaw in her hands, she leaned forward and kissed his tear away, breathing him in. 'Oh, I love you. I always have. Since the moment you knocked out a Viking in my honour.'

'Really?'

'*Really*, really. I just didn't believe in fairytales and happy-ever-afters. Didn't believe in happiness for myself at all. The right to dream beyond duty was drummed out of me when I was three feet tall. Duty was why I would marry—not for love. So, like a self-fulfilling prophecy, I ran years ago, when my heart screamed at me to stay and tell you who I was. I listened to my father and an age-old feud, ignoring my every instinct to come to you with our son. Duty would never bring happiness—my parents are proof of that—so when I discovered I was the key to your crown I ran scared again.'

She brushed his damp hair back from his temple, tucked one side behind his ear.

'But I think if we try we could have both. I promise I'm not running any longer. I'm here to stay—more than ready to be your Queen. Your wife and your lover too, if you want me. So what do you say?'

'Yes.'

Swooping in he came, and back down she went to the mattress, the heat of his body spilling over her.

'Yes. Yes, I'll marry you.' He wrapped her in his arms in a cherishing crush and breathed against her neck. 'I want it all too, Luciana. You'll always come first to me. *Always.* I love you so much. You've always owned my heart. Only you.'

A sigh feathered the aching wall of her throat and she closed her eyes as the last stain of doubt was erased. Replaced by the sweet sherbet-bright happiness that fizzled inside of her. If she'd heard him right, that was.

'I have?'

'Always,' he said, his lips moving over her skin.

For long moments they held on tight. Breathing. Loving. Calming. Trying to accept a dream beyond dreaming, a thing too precious ever to risk again. Then he was kissing her with exquisite annihilating tenderness and she was melting beneath his fervid ardour.

'Why else would I search for you for weeks, turn over every stone in Zurich looking for you, while my heart wouldn't beat and my lungs could barely breathe?'

She felt one fat tear trickle down the side of her face. 'Ah, Thane, why didn't you tell me?'

'I didn't want to give you that power over me again. Stupid to think I had any control over it at all. I even kidded myself I was only after my crown. That worked for…'

He hiked his shoulders and she felt the play of muscle against her palms.

'I don't know—maybe a day? I wish I'd told you that at the ice rink, instead of making it all about the throne. I was a coward.' Red scored his cheekbones. 'And now I'm rambling.'

She laughed at his newfound candour. 'No, you're not—you're talking, and I love it. It's wonderful. That's what I need.'

'To share. You told me. See? I do listen to you, Luciana, I just… At first I thought I was doing the right thing. And, *Dios*, I should have asked you to marry me, but I didn't want to hear your voice say no. I *was* silencing you, and that made me as bad as my father. Black. Twisted up inside. I kept having these visions of you hurting yourself, like my mother used to, and—'

'Hey, look at me. *Never* going to happen. She wasn't well, Thane. And that was your father's doing—it had nothing to do with you. You're nothing like him. You're a heroic man in *here*.' She placed her palm over his heart…a heart that thumped in tandem with hers. 'Will you tell me about her one day?'

Closing his eyes, he rested his brow against hers. 'One day soon. Just not today. Let me enjoy having you back in my arms.'

'Okay.' That was plenty good enough for her. 'Just promise me you'll keep talking. If you're hurting I need to know, so I can be there for you. In the silence I'd convinced myself we were doomed. When you don't share with me my mind runs wild. You were at the castle, trying to keep us safe, and I was picturing you with mistresses, you know?'

His eyes sprang open and his head reared back. '*Que*? You are *crazy*, Luce.'

'Yeah, well, one day I'll tell you about my childhood. Or, better yet, I'll sleep out one night and not bother telling you what I'm doing and who—'

'Like hell you will.'

'Need I say more?'

He growled. 'I didn't think of that. But I swear you'll see a snowball in hell before I ever take a mistress.' He brushed his lips over hers, back and forth. Teasing. Tormenting. 'Only you.'

Then he began to rain lush, moist kisses down her throat in a golden trail.

'I've been the only lover in your life, yes?'

Blood thrumming, she writhed against the satin sheets. 'Y…Yes, you know that.'

Nudging at the lace covering her breast, he swirled his hot breath over her skin as he murmured, 'And you are the only lover in mine. There has only been you and there will only ever be you.'

Blame it on the havoc being unleashed on her body, but it took her a second to catch on—and then she pushed at his shoulders to gauge his expression. 'You mean you haven't slept with anyone since *me*?'

Nonchalance made his shrug loose, as if he didn't see the big deal. 'No. It felt wrong. Like I was betraying my heart.'

'But…but you're a *man*.'

A laugh rumbled from the depths of his chest. 'I am *so* glad you've noticed that, angel.'

'And you're…*hot*.'

His eyes smouldered along with his smile as he towered above her, dominating her world, as always.

'I am *hot* for you right now,' he growled, with such sexual gravitas she shivered. 'Hot enough to show you exactly how much of a man I am.'

His sinful tongue licked across the seam of her lips in silent entreaty and she fisted his hair and surrendered, holding him to her as that black magic enthralled her.

It was the distant tinkle of glasses and music that pierced her lust fog.

'Oh, Lord, Thane, our guests! You have to get dressed. We're getting married on the beach in…' Lifting her head, she peeked at the bedside clock. 'Crikey—seven minutes.'

And she wouldn't like to guess what she looked like. Their wide eyes met and they both burst out laughing like lovestruck teenagers.

'Seriously, though, I was thinking this private ceremony could be for us. We'll have a big splash at the cathedral, before your coronation. It will give my father time to come round too. We need peace between our houses, Thane. I want us to end this feud. You and I. Together.'

'Whatever you want—whatever makes you happy. I can be nice to your father. For thirty seconds at least.'

'Make it sixty-nine and I'll pay you in kind.'

He growled like a virile feral wolf. 'I'm having you back in this bed within two hours.'

'Then move it.'

Tornado-style, they whirled around the room, yanking suit hangers and buttoning shirts and shoving feet into shoes. Before she knew it they were at the door.

'You look indecently gorgeous, Prince Thane. I adore you in this black Armani. All dissolute and wicked. How do *I* look?'

He pointed his index finger north. 'Your halo is wonky.'

Her smile exploded into laughter. 'You mean my tiara?'

'*Si.* Not that I care. To me you look perfect. A debauched angel.'

'And I bet you like that, huh?'

'Of course,' he drawled.

She was beaming—she knew it. 'Okay, Romeo, are you ready to marry your Juliet?'

'I am ready to marry *you*, Luciana. To finally make you mine.'

She laced her hand through his and he gripped it with warm fingers and devout love and the promise of unaccountable tomorrows.

'Then let's do it. Let's make our destiny our own.'

* * * * *

HARLEQUIN®

Presents®

Revenge and seduction intertwine…

Harlequin Presents welcomes you to the
world of The Chatsfield:
Synonymous with style, spectacle…and scandal!

SHEIKH'S SCANDAL by *Lucy Monroe* May 2014

PLAYBOY'S LESSON by *Melanie Milburne* June 2014

SOCIALITE'S GAMBLE by *Michelle Conder* July 2014

BILLIONAIRE'S SECRET by *Chantelle Shaw* August 2014

TYCOON'S TEMPTATION by *Trish Morey* September 2014

RIVAL'S CHALLENGE by *Abby Green* October 2014

REBEL'S BARGAIN by *Annie West* November 2014

HEIRESS'S DEFIANCE by *Lynn Raye Harris* December 2014

Step into the gilded world of The Chatsfield!
Where secrets and scandal lurk behind
every door…

Reserve your room!

HP132492